THE ANCHOR CROSS

Second Edition

Richard G. Edwards

COVER PHOTO

The photograph on the front cover, taken by the author, is the actual Cumberland Gap through which Daniel Boone passed in 1775 and the Samuel Howard family in 1796.

Acknowledgements

I received great encouragement to write this book from my good friend, fellow Harlan High School graduate, and author Bill J. Looney. I asked several people to review the book, including Mrs. Tracy Forester, Dr. Bill Green, Mr. Jack Sterling, Dr. August Peters and his son Dr. Carl Peters, and my wife Carolyn. I truly appreciate each of them taking the time and effort required to read the book and make suggestions, corrections, and comments.

Dedication

This book is dedicated to our son Richard Lange Edwards. Langie left this world at the tender age of 4 to go to a far better place. I look forward to being with him throughout eternity.

1.

It was hot and humid on the trail, as expected in August. The Reverend Karl Seibert and his wife Mary were delighted to have successfully passed through the Cumberland Gap with the wagon train headed West. Although originally there were two other wagons that had planned to accompany the Seiberts to Mount Pleasant, those two had decided at the last minute to stay with the wagon train headed West. So several miles after clearing the Gap, the Seiberts said their farewells and set out Northeast to Mount Pleasant.

Mount Pleasant had been settled in 1796 by Samuel Howard and his family. The Howards and the Seiberts had become friends after first meeting in Williamsburg in 1792. Howard had talked at length with Reverand Seibert about the beauty, resources, and potential of the Appalachian area, and after settling in Mount Pleasant had two years later written to Reverand Seibert asking him to consider coming to Mount Pleasant to establish a church. After much thought and prayer, the Reverend Seibert decided that he was called to follow the request of Samuel Howard to move to Mount Pleasant and to there start a church.

The going was tough. The trail Reverend Seibert and Mary were following was very difficult at times to even make out. It followed the river, but the trees and brush in most places made the trail virtually impossible to discern. Samuel Howard had mailed a map describing the trail from Cumberland Gap to his recently settled Mount Pleasant. The map had indicated that Mount Pleasant was about 30 miles Northeast of the trail through Cumberland Gap going West. So it was anticipated to take maybe 3 days, since only about 10 miles could be covered in a day on the rugged trail. The Reverend and his wife were now two days into this last leg of their long trip.

Karl Seibert was from a family of ministers. His father had been pastor of a church in Bremerhaven, Germany for 50 years. His grandfather was also a minister. Karl and been born and grew up in Bremerhaven and followed under his father's guidance to become a minister. Bremerhaven is located on the shores of the North Sea, and Karl had spent his youth enjoying and admiring the sea. Great lengths of time were spent fishing, boating, and swimming in the sea. And the lure of travel across the sea was always on Karl's young mind.

As Karl and Mary settled in for the evening they had

made a camp fire for cooking, and Mary was preparing their meal as Karl relaxed after another hard day on the trail. Karl was resting beside a large tree, sitting with his back to the tree and thinking about how far he had come on his journey from Bremerhaven. As he thought, he absently felt of the beautiful golden cross that he always kept on a leather necklace about his neck. He knew the cross was special. His father had given it to him before he left on his journey to Williamsburg. The cross had been passed down for generations. There were many stories about the cross, and Karl had heard these from both his father and grandfather. Not only was the cross beautifully proportioned and made of purest gold, but there had been many occurrences where those wearing the cross had encountered assistance that defied explanation. Karl had listened to such stories from his father and grandfather throughout his youth. Young Karl was always fascinated by such stories, but could not really comprehend their significance until that day at Williamsburg.

Williamsburg was founded as the capital of the Virginia colony in 1699. The town, located between the James and York rivers, is not far inland from the mouth of the Chesapeake Bay and Atlantic ocean. Upon reaching age 25, Karl Seibert made the decision to travel to the "new world" to preach the word. After a difficult voyage, he arrived in Virginia in 1790. He had previously been in contact with a fellow minister that had proceeded him from Bremerhaven to Virginia, and had been taken in by this friend and had assisted him in his ministerial duties at the new church in Williamsburg. In 1792 Reverend Seibert met Samuel Howard, and the two of them became good friends. In 1798, at the age of 33 Karl met his future wife, Mary, and after a brief time the two became man and wife. Samuel Howard had talked many times with his good friend Karl about the lure of the new frontier and that he, Samuel, planned to travel through Cumberland Gap, following the trail first established by Daniel Boone in 1775, and to then turn Northeast in search of a suitable place to settle somewhere in the beautiful Appalachian mountains.

So it was that on one fine, fall day in 1795 Karl was walking in the woods around Williamsburg. He liked very much hiking through the hills, and especially in the fall when the leaves had turned and the beauty of nature was so appealing. It was a clear, sunny day, and the leaves were absolutely brilliant with color. Karl had hiked alone several miles from his home, and was in an area with high cliffs adjacent to the James River. Unaware, because it was covered by leaves, there was a crevice directly in his path. Karl was not looking where he was walking anyway, but rather was looking all around at the beauty of the fall foliage. He stepped into the leaves covering the crevice, and his left foot plunged into the opening and caused him to fall into the crevice which opened immediately into a cliff that towered about 100 yards above the rocky shore of the James River below. Karl was falling! He remembered being in free fall and quickly realized that his life was rapidly coming to an end! As he fell the cross he was wearing around his neck flew up into his face and he grabbed it with one hand. When he did, it was as though gravity no longer existed. He felt light as a feather, and felt his decent rapidly decrease. What was happening?? The next thing he knew he was standing on the shore of the James River!! The cross was still in his hand, and it felt quite warm. He looked down and saw that he was standing among sharp, jagged rocks on the shore of the river. What had happened?? Was he dreaming?? With his other hand he felt his head and then his body. They seemed normal. He spoke, and heard his voice. All seemed fine except for the sprain in his left foot that had passed into the crevice and caused his fall. Then he looked closely at the cross. It was called the Anchor Cross because of the shape of an anchor on the bottom portion of the cross. His father and grandfather had told him that the anchor portion symbolized that people should be anchored to their Lord who had died on the cross for them. They told him the cross had been passed down for many generations ... it's exact origin unknown. It was at this time that Karl realized the significance of the stories he had heard his father and grandfather tell about the cross. Indeed it was special! It had just somehow saved his life!

Karl and Mary married in 1798, and a few months after the marriage Karl received the letter from his friend Samuel Howard requesting him to join him in the settlement at Mount Pleasant.

As Karl sat leaning against the tree awaiting Mary's evening meal, he decided he would bathe before dinner. The river was only yards away from their wagon. Karl told Mary his plans, and before he left he removed the Anchor Cross from around his neck and placed it in a secret compartment below the wagon seat. He was always very much afraid of losing or damaging the cross. Karl valued the cross with his life, and had built the hidden compartment carefully under the wagon seat as a place to store the cross when he was not wearing it. So once the cross was stored, Karl went to the river to bathe.

Settlers had found most Indians living in the area friendly. The Cherokees were very friendly, and would share furs and food with the settlers, and would be of assistance frequently. However, there were roving bands of Indians that were far less than friendly. Unfortunately for Karl and Mary, it was the latter that they encountered that evening.

As Karl bathed in the river he relished the coolness of the clear water and the sound of the birds. A loud scream broke his tranquility. He recognized the scream as coming from Mary at the wagon. He rushed out of the water, pulled on his pants, and then ran toward their camp. He had just gotten to the camp in time to see Mary slump into the camp fire with an arrow in her back. Two Indians were rummaging through their belongings in the wagon, but before he could act he felt the thud of a tomahawk hit his chest. As he slumped to the ground his last thought was that he was not wearing the Anchor Cross.

Present Time

2.

Kentucky was granted statehood in 1792. Mount Pleasant was established by Samuel Howard in 1796 as a settlement in Southeastern Kentucky. The area surrounding Mount Pleasant became Harlan County in 1819, and in 1820 there was a transaction recorded wherein Harlan County purchased 12 acres of land from Samuel Howard for $5 for the purpose of establishing residential lots in the newly named town of Harlan, previously called Mount Pleasant. From these beginnings Harlan began to grow as the county seat of Harlan County, Kentucky.

"Sounds like Snake Potter is at it again,", Rosie said, "Just got another call from their neighbor saying he could hear glass breaking at Snake's house!"

Rosie Cain was a deputy in the Harlan County Sheriff's office located in downtown Harlan at 210 E. Central Street. Her duties mainly were to function as clerk for Sheriff J. Bert Sterling. Rosie was 35 years old, attractive, and happily married.

"Hate to say it, Rosie, but I guess I'll have to pay Snake another visit," Said Sheriff Sterling. "We sure waste a lot of taxpayer dollars on him!"

J. Bert Sterling had been Harlan County Sheriff now for about 15 years. He was 48 years old, and had established himself as an honest, hardworking, dedicated law enforcement officer since beginning as a deputy when he was 18 years old. The people of Harlan County overwhelming reelected Bert every time his name was on the ballot. He was liked and trusted. Bert had never married .... his law enforcement career occupied his time completely. He was tall at 6 feet and 2 inches, slim, and considered handsome. Many single ladies in Harlan were always seeking his companionship!

"Better strap your gun on before going," said Rosie, "old Snake might do anything when he's drunk. And you can bet your bottom dollar he is drunk!"

Bert was already grabbing his holster and coat. "Thanks for the advice Rosie, but you know I can take care of myself"

Bert always was very particular about his appearance. Anytime he was out in public he wanted to present a good image of the Sheriff's office. Too many stereotypes of fat, sloppy Southern law enforcement officials were lodged in people's minds, and Bert did not want to further that image for Harlan County. The history of the county was bad enough already. First thing many people thought when Harlan was mentioned was "Bloody Harlan", owing to the killings associated with disputes largely between coal mining company operators and coal miners back around the 1920s, 30s, and 40s. And Bert was doing all he could to change that image.

Snake Potter lived about 10 miles South of Harlan near the town of Wallins. No one knew Snake's real first name .... he had just been called "snake" all his life, and everyone knew the reason was because he was mean as a snake! His wife Carolyn and young son Kylie lived with Snake. Their home was a small old dilapidated wood-frame home located in a remote, wooded area. There were a couple of other similar homes situated along the Cumberland river within earshot of the Potter home. The closest home belonged to a fellow that Snake had never liked, and he was constantly complaining to Sheriff Sterling about Snake's behavior.

Bert arrived at the Potter residence around noon. As soon as he opened his car door he could hear Snake shouting, cussing, and throwing things inside the house.

When Bert knocked on the door there was a silence in the home, and then Snake opened the door, saw the Sheriff, and uttered a profanity under his alcohol saturated breath.

"Morning Snake," said the Sheriff, "Been gettin reports again bout you being too rowdy! Just had to make sure that you and your family are o.k."

Bert looked inside the house and saw Snake's wife Carolyn cowering in a corner of the house with her 10 year old son Kylie. It looked like Carolyn had a cut on her face, and her dress was torn on the left shoulder. Kylie looked very frightened. They said nothing.

"None of your damn business Bert", Snake growled

"Beg to differ, Snake," said the Sheriff. "Protecting the citizens of this fine county is my sworn duty, and from the looks of things the missus and son are in need of protection! I think you've been drinking too much of that shine again".

Snake quickly grabbed a kitchen knife off the table beside him and lunged it at Bert's chest. His move was both predictable and clumsy, and Bert easily deflected the knife with one hand while jerking his knee into Snake's groin. Snake released the knife and fell to his knees, screaming in pain. Bert grabbed his handcuffs and quickly had them on Snake. He then jerked him to his feet and took him to his car and placed him in the secured back seat, and then returned to the house to talk with Carolyn.

"Carolyn, I feel so sorry for you and Kylie. Snake's drinking just seems to keep getting worse. I know he abuses you and Kylie when he's drunk, and I know you don't want to place charges against him, but I'm really concerned that one of these days he may really do some serious damage to you or your son!"

Carolyn's eyes were red and moist. She seemed to have a slight cut above her eye. Carolyn was 30 years old, and remained attractive. She worked as a teller at the Miners Bank in Harlan, and could avoid Snake most of the time during the work week. Kylie was in 5th grade at Wallins elementary, and after school each day walked to his grandmother's home just a few blocks from the school to stay until Carolyn picked him up on her way home from work. Most evenings Snake did not show up at home, thankfully. The weeks ends, like now, were the problem.

Carolyn had excelled in school, and after graduating from Harlan High School had secured a job at the Harlan Miners Bank. Calvin Brown, the bank's president, had liked Carolyn and had trained her to be a teller at the bank. Her job performance there was excellent.

Carolyn had met Snake just after finishing High School. He had dropped out of school and was working at an automobile junk yard and living with his parents. Although his behavior was at times bazaar, Carolyn thought she could change him for the better if given the chance, and she did like him. After a few months of courting, the two were married about the time that Carolyn found she was pregnant. After Kylie was born, Snake's behavior just seemed to get worse by the day....as did his drinking. And Carolyn found herself trapped in a position of having to support and care for both Snake and Kylie, and to try and survive the now common drunken rages of her husband.

"I just don't know how much longer I can go on like this, Bert," Carolyn whispered through trembling lips. "I do love my husband.....he's only a problem when he drinks. But that's certainly gotten a lot worse recently. I still keep thinking I can change him, but I really just don't know if that is even possible.".

Bert looked with sympathy at Carolyn and said, "Yeah, I know. And I wish I had a good answer for you. But right now all I can do is lock him up and let him sleep it off. You and Kylie might want to go to your mothers tomorrow and finish off the weekend. Then you'll probably be o.k. to come back home Monday when Snake's at work."

Carolyn nodded, and hugged Kylie. Bert left to deliver Snake to jail.

3.

"Snake, I can't believe you let the Sheriff kick you in the balls!" said Bad Eye. "I sure wish I could have seen that!"

"Bert just got the drop on me," Snake said. "I probably was a little slow. I had drunk almost a quart of our shine .... wonder I was even able to stand up! There'll be another day ... I'll get even, you can damn well make book on that."

Snake was at his job at Bad Eye's Junk Yard, located between Harlan and Wallins. It was Monday and Snake had sobered up over the weekend and gotten out of jail. Sheriff Sterling had once again warned him that he better lay off causing trouble for Carolyn and Kylie. The words passing in one of Snake's ears and out the other. After getting out of jail Snake caught a ride to Bad Eye's for work.

Bad Eye Cawood had inherited his father's junk yard. It was almost impossible to make a living with it, so Bad Eye had hired Snake and two others to help around the junk yard, but more importantly to help him make moonshine. Bad Eye got his name when as a kid he had a disease that left him blind in his right eye. He wore an eye patch, and had been called Bad Eye all his life. Jones Anderson and Billie Lingal worked for Bad Eye along with Snake. They were also local boys and had gone to school with Snake. Bad Eye was in his mid fifties, and the other three were each about 30 years old. They had a spot in the woods about a mile from the junk yard where they had erected a still and worked most nights producing moonshine. The demand (and money) was higher for the moonshine in Knoxville, Tennessee than around Southeastern Kentucky, so they had modified a pick-up truck with special tanks to haul the shine to Knoxville, a distance of about 100 miles from Harlan. They generally made two trips a week to Knoxville, one on Tuesday and one on Friday. They took turns making the trips, which took about 5 hours round-trip to drive to Knoxville, unload the shine, and then drive back to Harlan.

Bad Eye said, "O.K. you three, listen up. We need to talk. We been doing o.k. with our "Thunder Road" business, but we ain't gettin rich! I'm pushing 60 and don't have savings or any retirement but social security. So I been thinking about a plan to get us all enough money so that we can forget this junk yard and moonshinin and be able to retire in the lap of luxury. And you three are only about 30 years old ..... so you'd have a lot more retirement ahead of you than I would!"

Snake looked at Bad Eye and said, " Sounds illegal to me Bad Eye."

Billie said, "Hell Snake, we never did do nothing that was legal. Even most of the parts we buy and sell here at the junk yard are from stolen cars, and I sure as hell never heard of no legal moonshine!"

Jones had listened to the other three and said, "Bad Eye's the brains of this outfit. I say if he has come up with a good plan that will put us all on easy street we damn well ought to hear him out". Snake and Billie both slowly nodded their heads. Snake said, "Bad Eye, what you got in mind?".

Bad Eye leaned back in his chair and fired up a cigar, blowing big clouds of smoke toward the other three. After a bit he said, "I may well be the brains in this outfit, but even a stupid man would agree if you want money you go to a bank!"

Snake said, "Bad Eye, I don't think any one of us could qualify for a loan!" Billie and Jones snickered.

Bad Eye said, "Wasn't thinking about taking out no loan. Thinking more about relieving the bank of all its money in one fell swoop.".

Snake said, "Now just how you thinkin about going about that? Last time I checked they had a big vault and security all around the banks. They take a dim view of people trying to get their money. Sounds to me like a ticket to the big house rather than retirement.". Billie and Jones grunted.

"I have a plan," said Bad Eye. "We ain't gonna get caught, and we gonna relieve them of all their money. I figure we'll walk with at least a million each. That should be enough for a real fancy retirement in the Bahamas. Be a end of all this junk and shine business!".

It was real quiet for the next couple of minutes, then Snake said, "I don't object to an early retirement, but I want to hear all the details.". Billie and Jones nodded.

"Just a few things I'm still working on," said Bad Eye, "and then I'll meet with all of you to go over the plan. Today I just wanted to gauge your interest. Are you in?".

There was another quiet period, and then each of the three slowly nodded.

Bad Eye rocked back in his chair, put his feet up on his desk, and blew a big smoke ring!

4.

About a half mile from Bad Eye's Junk Yard, between Wallins and Harlan, was Maggard's Grocery. It was a small building, evenly divided into two rooms, each 35 feet long and 25 feet deep. The building was a wood frame with siding and was about 40 years old. As you entered the front door you were immediately in the grocery store. The walls were lined with shelves of groceries, and there were 4 aisles of snack food racks and refrigerated drinks and food. At the far right side there was a counter for check out with a cash register. Behind the counter was a chair. In the chair sat Fatso Chapel, the store clerk. Fatso spent the majority of his time watching a small television that sat on the counter beside the cash register.

The back room was accessed through a door in the middle of the grocery's back wall. The back room was the office of Pretty Boy Maggard, owner of the store and the chief drug dealer in Eastern Kentucky. He had spent some money on his office. It had one very large desk, behind which Pretty Boy spent most of his time. There was a large flat screen television wall mounted. A refrigerator, microwave, three large file cabinets, and a computer desk. In addition there was a small desk at the other side of the room that belonged to Trigger Green.

Trigger was Pretty Boy's "bag man". His primary duty was to collect and deliver monies as directed by Pretty Boy. He also served as body guard for Pretty Boy. Trigger got his nickname when he was in grade school. At age 12 his father had given him a twenty two caliber rifle and he spent a great deal of his time hunting and shooting the rifle. He quickly advanced to rifles and pistols of larger caliber .... so all his friends labeled him "Trigger". Now at 35 years old many said that Trigger was the best shot in Harlan County.

The grocery store was just a "front" for Maggard's drug operation. On a given day the grocery store would have maybe 10 customers, and it was only open from 8 am till 5 pm Monday through Saturday. Fatso's main duty was to carefully watch anyone entering the store and determine quickly if they were friend or foe. Most all those coming for groceries were regulars, and Fatso knew them. An occasional motorist would stop for something cold to drink and/or a snack, and these folks Fatso had to carefully evaluate whether or not they might have other intentions. Also, there were closed-circuit tv cameras in both the outside parking lot and in the grocery store that permitted viewing in the back room.

Mrs. Johnson lived just a short walk from Maggard's grocery, and was a regular customer.

"How you doin today Fatso," said Mrs. Johnson as she checked out a few groceries.

"Bout the same as usual Mrs. Johnson." Fatso said. "I see you buyin a can of beans .... you know why they put 239 beans in a can?'

"Why Fatso, I never thought about it .... why do they put 239 beans in a can?"

"Cause if they put in one more they'd be two forty!" Fatso said and roared laughing!
Mrs. Johnson just looked at Fatso, took her groceries and left. Fatso was laughing so hard he had tears rolling down his cheeks. He loved to tell jokes.

Soon after Mrs. Johnson left the store the door opened and in walked Sheriff J. Bert Sterling and his deputy Ape Cornett. Ape was about 10 years younger than Bert, and got his nickname because of his very long and apelike arms and body. He was very lean and muscular. He had been with Bert since Bert became sheriff about 15 years ago.

"Morning Fatso, need to see Pretty Boy .... push the button" said the sheriff.

"Howdy sheriff, Ape. I know Pretty Boy'll be delighted

to see you again .... go right in," said Fatso as he pressed the button below the cash register to unlock the door going to the back room.

Bert and Ape walked into the back room. Pretty Boy sat behind his desk. He and Trigger had seen the sheriff and Ape enter the grocery on their closed-circuit tv. Trigger was standing beside the computer desk looking intently at the sheriff.

"Well, well, if ain't the sheriff of Harlan County and deputy dog," said Pretty Boy. "Must be something important up to bring you to my humble establishment."

"Just wanted to pass along some information to you Pretty Boy. There was a bad car wreck last night just across Pine Mountain on 421. Guy driving was flying low and lost it around one of the curves and met a tree. The tree won. The guy was pronounced dead on arrival by the ambulance driver," said the sheriff.

"What's that got to do with me sheriff?" said Pretty Boy.

"Well, the ole boy was carrying a bag that had about $200,000 in cash in it, and there was a note addressed to you," Bert said. "Unfortunately, the note, signed by someone named Jim, only said something to the effect that it had been a good month and had nothing that would stand up in court for me to charge you with, but I thought you might like to know. Unless his next of kin shows up to claim the money, which I seriously doubt, then the county will be $200,000 richer"

Both Pretty Boy and Trigger had glum looks on their faces, and just nodded.

After a minute of silence Bert said, "One of these days Pretty Boy you're going to screw-up and I'll be able to bust you good. And you too Trigger."

Trigger got a slight grin on his face, but Pretty Boy showed no reaction.

The Sheriff and Ape turned and left.

After watching on the closed circuit tv the sheriff's car leave their parking lot, Pretty Boy looked at Trigger and said "Damn, there goes $200,000! The boys up in Floyd County sure did have a good month .... too bad they didn't have enough sense to send a driver that could keep the car on the road."

"Yeah," said Trigger. "Old Big Jim in Floyd is not going to like hearing about losing that money. And it cuts into our take too. But I guess it's just a part of doing business!"

Pretty Boy had started out in the rackets as a kid growing marijuana in the remote hollers of Harlan County. He was smart, and he was able, for the most part, to avoid the law. He saved his money, and after several years was able to buy the grocery store and start to expand his business. He made contact with other marijuana growers in Eastern Kentucky and soon had deals struck that set him up to "launder" their money. The large amounts of cash that accumulated from selling marijuana was a major problem for the dealers unless they could get the money into bank accounts that would not be noticed by law enforcement agencies. Pretty Boy had been fortunate to know a banker in Knoxville that specialized in such transactions. So over the years Pretty Boy's business had grown to mainly be one of laundering drug money for most all the drug dealers in Eastern Kentucky. They would send Pretty Boy their cash. Pretty Boy would take a 10% cut, and then credit the other 90% to the dealer.

So Pretty Boy received large amounts of cash monthly. He knew that the sheriff would find some pretense to raid his business and find any cash he might keep there (and that could be big trouble with both the sheriff and the IRS), so he devised a system whereby he had rented two large safe deposit boxes in the Miners Bank at Harlan to hold the cash until he could get it to the banker in Knoxville. Pretty Boy had given lots of thought in trying to minimize his chances of getting caught, and had decided that he would only chance one trip every 3 months to deliver the cash from his safe deposit boxes to the Knoxville banker.

On average, Pretty Boy was now up to about 20 deposits per month from drug dealers in his Eastern Kentucky network. In order to avoid suspicion at the Miners Bank because of so many visits to his safe deposit boxes, Pretty Boy had cultivated a teller at the bank, one Miss Julie Lacey, to assist in his operation. Miss Lacey had responsibility at the bank for the vault, and for allowing customers access to their safe deposit boxes. Pretty Boy had arranged for a special "photo session" when Miss Lacey had met one of Pretty Boy's associates at a party one evening, and after a lot of drinks had agreed to a motel visit. The motel room had previously been set up with a hidden camera, and pictures had been taken of Miss Lacey in very compromising positions. When confronted with these pictures along with an offer of $500 for each assistance in making drops in safe deposit boxes, Miss Lacey readily agreed. So the arrangement was that every time a delivery was made to Pretty Boy at Maggard's grocery he would shortly send Trigger to town with the cash tied in bundles and placed in a large woman's pocketbook and left on the passenger seat of his car. Trigger would send a text message to Miss Lacey telling her a delivery should be picked up during her lunch break. Trigger would always park his car in the same area on Central Street close to the bank, and Miss Lacey would then walk by the car and use the remote that Trigger had given her to unlock the car and to remove the pocketbook that contained the cash. Her $500 fee was in the pocketbook separate from the bundled cash. Miss Lacey would never carry her own pocketbook when going to retrieve the drop, so she would simply remove the large pocketbook from the car, put it around her arm, and proceed down the street. When she got back to the bank after lunch she would choose a time when no others were in the vault, and go in with the bundled cash covered on a cart that she used for vault cleaning. When inside the vault she would use the key given her by Trigger and the required matching bank key that she had to open the lock box and then deposit the bundled cash. Then only once every 3 months would Trigger come to the bank and get all the cash out of their boxes and make the delivery to the Knoxville banker who would then, after deducting his 10%, transfer the balance into offshore accounts previously established for Pretty Boy and for each of the Eastern Kentucky drug dealers. Pretty Boy included an accounting sheet with each Knoxville deposit that indicated the dollar amount that should be credited for each of the approximately 20 dealers plus the amount to be credited for his 10%.

The operation had worked flawlessly for years.

5.

Kylie had always been a good kid. Fortunately for him, he took after his mother and not his father. It had been a hard life, however, because of his father's constant drinking. Kylie could not remember a time when he and his mother were not in fear of his father. It was always especially bad on the weekends, but even during the week Snake would often come stumbling home drunk after work and talk terrible and sometimes hit Carolyn. On those weekdays when he came home sober he usually just demanded that Carolyn fix him something to eat and then sat in his chair and watched tv. Snake just never showed love or even affection toward his wife and son.

During school days Kylie walked to his grandmother's house to stay after school until his mom could pick him up on her way home after work. Everyone called Kylie's grandmother "Mawie". Mawie's husband had passed away from cancer many years before Kylie was born. Mawie's home in Wallins was a very neat old brick home where she had lived since getting married. Kylie had some games he left at Mawies, and he sometimes watched television with his grandmother, but usually he liked to play outside if the weather permitted.

Today was a lovely spring day, and after school Kylie had walked to Mawies, and then decided to explore the woods. He loved to explore! His ten year old mind was very inquisitive, and he always enjoyed discovering new flowers, small animals, and any junk or relics he came across. So on that day Kylie left grandmothers and started hiking. He liked to explore areas that were off the beaten trails, so he ventured along the river bank for about a mile, and then turned into a heavily wooded area to see what he might discover. It was almost like a jungle. The vegetation was already in bloom, and everything looked so inviting to Kylie. After about 15 minutes of plowing through the flora Kylie came across something sticking up out of the ground. It was round and looked like a wheel. As he ran his fingers over it's rusty surface he decided it indeed was some kind of wheel. He tried pulling it out of the ground, and when he did he found it was attached to some kind of old rotten wooden board, and at the other end of the board he saw what looked like another wheel laying on its side. Oh boy!! Hidden treasure, he thought. He scraped the dirt and leaves off the board as best he could, and then noticed that it looked like the board had been burned....it seemed charred on its edges. It finally gave way to his pulling, and then he noticed that there was something on the bottom side of the board. He turned the board over and was excited to see a small box attached to the board's bottom that had also been burned, but was still intact. One end of the box was hinged and secured in place by a rusty lock. As he grasped the lock he pulled and the rusty, dilapidated hinges gave way and the end of the box came off. Kylie peered into the now open end of the small box. To his shock he saw something laying inside the box that was shiny and almost seemed to glow! Slowly he reached into the box and grabbed one end of the object and pulled it out. Astonished, he looked at the beautiful golden cross. He had never seen anything as beautiful in all his life! He immediately knew he had indeed found buried treasure!! The bottom of the cross had the shape of an anchor, and the top of the cross had a leather neck strap attached. He placed the strap over his head and wore the cross around his neck. Just wait until he told Mawie, his mom, and the kids at school about this!! He had found hidden treasure!!

With the cross around his neck, Kylie walked a few feet over to a tree and sat down beside it to think. This was so exciting he could hardly stand it. He carefully examined the cross. It was heavy for its size, and so brilliant and gold! He scuffled his right foot as he was about to stand up and noticed his foot hit something. He looked and saw what looked like a stick attached to something. He used his foot to clear away the dirt from around the stick, and then was shocked when he followed the stick into the ground to see what appeared to be bones. Clearing more of the ground around the bones he suddenly removed dirt from a skull that looked large enough to be human!

His sudden joy had turned to terror! Was this some kind of burial ground? And what did the cross have to do with it? Now Kylie was really scared. He turned back toward the direction he had come and walked quickly back out of the woods to the path. He then sat down on the ground. He wanted to think about what he had discovered and what he should do. He looked again at the beautiful golden cross around his neck. He carefully removed it, wrapped the neck strap around it, and placed it in his pocket. He knew he had to tell about his discovery of the bones, but he wanted to keep the cross. So he decided to hide it for a while until he decided exactly what he wanted to do.

He started walking back down the path to his grandmothers.

6.

Preacher Puss was a 15 pound long haired grey tabby cat. She now made her home in the Harlan County Sheriff's office. Two years ago there was a fire in a rural church in Harlan County. After the fire department got there the building was gone, but remarkably, the firemen heard very loud screams coming from a back room which was totally engulfed in smoke, but had been spared from the fire. When the firemen got into the room they followed the screams to a corner where they found the cat. Even after it's rescue, the cat continued to scream for about an hour until they got her to the vet. He had then tranquilized her so he could do an examination to determine any problems. After pronouncing her sound, the now quieted cat was returned to the firemen. The firemen had inquired of the pastor at the burned out church about the cat, but the pastor said he knew of no cat that belonged around the church and he guessed the cat had somehow gotten into the back room when a door had been left open. None of the firemen were able to adopt the cat, so they took her to the sheriff's office.

Rosie Cain had loved animals all her life. She had two dogs at home, and when the fireman walked into the sheriff's office holding the big long haired grey cat Rosie just fell in love again. There was no way that cat was going to be homeless. When the fireman left, Rosie told Ape to watch the office, she was headed for Wal-Mart to get cat supplies! When she got back she had a good supply of cat food and treats as well as a large pillowed bed, a cat box, large bag of cat litter, and food and water bowls. She made a home for the cat in the corner of the office that was behind her desk and had watched lovingly over the cat ever since.

The name for the cat was established when the fireman told Rosie the story of how they heard the cat screaming in the church. Rosie immediately declared the cat Preacher Puss.

Preacher Puss loved the sheriff's office, and was soon known to most all the folks that came to the office. Everyone always gave her an affectionate pet, and she always rubbed against them and purred and meowed. She did have one particular peculiarity. Apparently she hated guns. This was first discovered when on the day she was settling into her new home Ape removed his pistol from its holster and was going to clean it. At the time Preacher Puss was sitting on Ape's desk with her tail swishing back and forth, eyes closed, and purring contently. When Ape pulled the hammer back on his pistol to make sure the chamber was clear the click caused Preacher Puss to open one eye enough to see

Ape with the gun. Then next thing Ape knew Preacher Puss was clinging to his arm just above the hand holding the gun, digging her claws into Ape and screaming at the top of her lungs. Good thing there was no bullet in the chamber ..... Ape immediately jumped up with Preacher Puss still clinging to his arm. As soon as he dropped the gun the cat jumped down and went over to her bed, sat down and went to sleep. Everyone got a good laugh out of it .... except for Ape. He wore band-aids on his arm for several days. Since then no one held a gun in the sheriff's office.

"I'm not going to lose $200,000!" said Big Jim. "I hated that Marty got killed in that wreck, but he did it to himself! Slick, I want you to drive down to Harlan and pay a visit to the sheriff's office. I know they have our money in their evidence room, and all you need to do is walk in there when you know there are no others there and force a deputy into the evidence room and get our money. Then do whatever with the deputy, and get out of there and hightail it back here. Then we'll worry about getting it back to Pretty Boy.".

"But Big Jim how do I know when the sheriff's office don't have anyone in it?" asked Slick.

"How come I get all the stupid ones," said Big Jim. "Hell Slick, all you got to do is hang around outside the office until you can't see anyone else in there through the window, and then do your thing. It ain't rocket science!"

The sheriff's office, located in downtown Harlan on Central Street consisted of 4 large rooms. The first room, the one encountered as you entered through the outside door, was a reception room which consisted of a long desk behind which Rosie worked, a small desk on one side of the room where Ape worked when in the office, and a refreshment desk on the other side of the room that had a coffee maker, a small refrigerator, and microwave. The next room back was the sheriff's office and bathroom. The third room was the evidence and storage room, and the fourth room was a small holding facility where up to 4 people could be held for short periods of time, and later transported to county jail if required.

Because Preacher Puss enjoyed looking outside through a window, Ape had constructed a wooden shelf high up on the wall next to the outside door. By jumping on Ape's desk Preacher Puss could then leap on up to the shelf and lay and look through the window outside. In addition, anyone coming in the front door could, if they were familiar with Preacher Puss, reach up to their right and give her a pet. She approved of this arrangement greatly, and always was waiting for someone to come through the door.

Slick arrived at 9 am and parked on Central Street across from the entrance to the sheriff's office, and watched. At about 9:45 sheriff J. Bert Sterling and Deputy Rosie Cain came out of the office and headed down the street. Only one other person had gone into the office, and that person came out soon after the sheriff and Rosie left. Slick got out of his car and walked up to the window beside the door to the sheriff's office. He peeked in and only saw a deputy watching tv behind the counter. He reached into his jacket and pulled out the revolver and then slowly opened the door.

After walking the couple of steps into the sheriff's office with his gun pointed in front of him, Slick's world went dark! Preacher Puss took one giant leap onto the top of Slick's head with the claws in all four feet digging into the top of his head. Her long hair and part of her tummy was over his face and her head was facing down Slick's back and screaming at the top of her lungs. Ape jumped up about a foot out of his chair and leaped across the desk and grabbed the gun before Slick could see to fire it. As soon as Ape had the gun and laid it on his desk Preacher Puss jumped back to his shelf and Ape jerked Slick's arms behind him and placed handcuffs on.

"What in the hell kind of animal is that?" said Slick, with blood trickling down all around his head.

"Name's Preacher Puss. And she don't like guns," said Ape.

"I'm gonna sue hell out of the county for this," Slick said.

"You can do that," said Ape, "just as soon as you get out of jail after answering to a whole slew of charges, including flourishing a deadly weapon, attempted murder, attempted robbery, assaulting a law officer, and anything else I can think of.".

The door opened again and in walked sheriff Sterling and Deputy Cain.

Bert said, "My word Ape, what's happened here?"

Ape said, "Bert, this man walked through the door with a gun drawn, and, as you know, Preacher Puss don't like guns. Before I could look up Preacher Puss was off his shelf onto this guy's head with all claws digging and both the man and Preacher Puss screaming. I was able to then grab the gun and handcuff him. I was just getting ready to take him to our holding cell.".

When Ape had taken Slick to the holding cell, Rosie asked, "Wonder what the guy wanted?"

Bert answered, "Can't be completely sure, but it'd be my guess he was sent here to try and get that $200,000 back that we're holding in the evidence room. But I know we'll never get it out of him, and probably will never be able to find out anything for sure. We really don't have a lot to hold him on, other than some gun charges."

Rosie nodded, and Preacher Puss purred. Rosie gave Preacher Puss a big pat!

7.

Kylie was in his bed. After dinner he had finished his homework, and Carolyn had given him his goodnight hug and kiss. His father had not gotten home yet. It had been two days since he had encountered the "buried treasure". He had kept the beautiful cross with him .... in his pants pocket during the days and in his pajama pocket at nights. He was so afraid someone would find it and he just had not decided yet who to tell about it's discovery and the human bones. Kylie was very worried. He could not get it out of his mind. But he didn't know what to do.

Suddenly he heard the front door slam and heavy footsteps. He knew his father was home. He next heard some loud shouting, and cursing, and then rapid footsteps followed by breaking glass. His mother's scream confirmed that his father was once again drunk and attacking his mother. He felt so sorry for his mother.

Kylie jumped out of bed and rushed toward the kitchen where the noise appeared to be coming from. Looking into the kitchen from the living room he could see that his father was towering over his mother. She was now sitting in a kitchen chair, and he was standing by her looking down at her face.

"I don't give a damn how late it is, when I get home I want to be fed," Snake said. "The least you can do is have me a meal waiting!".

From her position in the chair Carolyn said, "But honey, it's almost 10 o'clock and I just didn't think you were coming home.".

"Well, here I am and I'm hungry as a bear! Where's my food?" said Snake.

"I'll have to get something going, darling, and I'll have you a meal shortly," Carolyn said.

"That's not good enough. You should have it ready when I get here. I think I need to give you a little something that'll help you remember to always have my food ready." And with that Snake grabbed one of Kylie's baseball bats laying in a chair beside him, and raised the bat high above his head and started down with a blow to Carolyn's head that was sure to be devastating.

Before even he knew what was happening, Kylie ran and leaped between his father and mother with his hands raised. The baseball bat, coming down with all the force that Snake could put behind it, seemed to hit a rubber wall just before it reached Kylies outstretched arms.

The bat suddenly bounced back without any loss of force and struck Snake in the forehead. He slumped to the ground out cold. Carolyn and Kylie looked in disbelief, first at each other, and then at the prone figure of Snake on the floor. How had that happened?

Kylie suddenly felt heat coming from his pants pocket. He reached into the pocket and pulled out the beautiful golden cross. It was quite warm to his touch. Carolyn looked in awe at the cross.

"Kylie, what is that and where did you get it?" asked Carolyn

"I've been wanting to tell you mother, but I just didn't know how to explain it. I think now is the time!" Kylie said.

"I'm most anxious to hear," said Carolyn. "But I'm afraid you father might wake up and cause more problems. I think we should head for Mawie's for the evening. Hurry and get your school clothes for tomorrow and your toothbrush and meet me in the car .... we'll talk about your cross when we get to mothers.".

Carolyn and Kylie quickly made their way to the car and got underway to Mawie's house. Little did they know that Snake would not wake up till noon, and then with a world-class headache!

It was close to 11 pm when they arrived. Carolyn had used her cell phone to call ahead to tell her mother what had happened and that they were on their way to spend the night.

After arriving and getting big hugs from Mawie, the three got comfortable on the living room sofa, and Carolyn said, "O.K. Kylie, I think now would be a good time to hear about the beautiful and mysterious cross in your pocket.".

Kylie reached into his pocket and removed his treasure. His grandmother's eyes got large as saucers, and Carolyn looked once again in amazement!

"Two days ago after school I took a hike by the river, and then turned off the trail for a little ways," Kylie started. "I came upon an old rusty wheel stuck into the ground, and after pulling on it found it was attached to a board that had been burned. I pulled some more and the board finally came loose. I then saw another old wheel buried at the other end of the board. And when I was trying to get all the dirt off the board I felt something on it's back side. I turned it over and saw a little box-like thing that had an old rusty lock. I tugged on it and the hinges on the box broke. I looked inside and saw the cross. I pulled it out and then sat down beside a tree to look at it, and my foot hit something and when I looked I saw some bones. I cleared more dirt around the area and then saw this skeleton head ..... it looked big enough to be a human head!! I was really scared!! I didn't know what to do so I just put the cross in my pocket and went back to grannys. I knew I needed to tell someone, but was scared I would lose my cross. That's what happened."

Carolyn hugged Kylie and patted him on the head. Mawie nodded her head. They all were silent for a moment, and then Carolyn said, "Kylie, I feel like you will certainly be able to keep the cross, but we need to find out more about it and what the bones around it were. And we need to try to find out what caused the bat to bounce. What I would like to do is for us to visit Pastor Bell to show him the cross and get his advice on it and what we should do. Pastor Bell is quite a historian as well as a wonderful pastor, and I just bet he'll be able to shed a little light on your treasure. Would that be o.k. with you?"

Kylie nodded rapidly, "Yeah, I think that would be exactly the best thing to do. When do you think we might be able to meet with him?"

"Well, tomorrow is Saturday and I bet your father will be sleeping late, so after we spend the night here with Mawie why don't we plan to get up early and go over to the parsonage. Pastor Bell will likely be studying for the Sunday service, but he's always happy to take time to visit. Does that sound o.k. with you?"

"Great Mom, let's get some sleep!"

8.

After a day being held in the sheriff's office, Slick went before the county judge charged with several gun violations and attempted robbery. Slick's lawyer, on retainer from Big Jim, argued that Slick had just come to the sheriff's office to turn in the gun that he had found, and that he had no intention of robbery. He was just a citizen doing his duty, according to the lawyer. Since the sheriff had no evidence to the contrary, and since there was no conflict other than between Preacher Puss and Slick, the judge dismissed the charges and released Slick. Upon walking out of the court house Slick pulled his cell phone and called Big Jim, and was told to sit by the doughboy in front of the court house on Central Street until Big Jim got there from Floyd County to pick him up. Big Jim said they had unfinished business to take care of.

Fatso was sound asleep in his chair behind the counter at Maggard's grocery. No one had been in the store for the past hour and Fatso had stayed up late the night before watching wrestling on tv, and then he didn't sleep well when he did go to bed. He had dozed off in his chair about 15 minutes before Big Jim and Slick walked unnoticed through the front door. Big Jim saw Fatso deep in sleep in his chair with his hands clasped across his chest and snoring loudly.

Big Jim put a finger to his lips to indicate to Slick to be quiet, and tip-toed over to the counter beside Fatso. Big Jim then slammed down his right fist on the counter making a noise that caused Fatso to raise completely from his chair. While doing so Fatso passed gas .... he farted. And it was not one of those silent ones, it was a real cheek-flapper loud enough to reverberate off the walls! Big Jim and Slick both doubled over laughing, and Fatso's face turned red as a pickled-beet!

"You need some toilet paper Fatso?" said Big Jim

"Damn you Big Jim, why'd you have to go and do that?" said Fatso.

"To get even with you for all those corny jokes," Big Jim responded.

Slick had grabbed today's copy of the Harlan Daily Enterprise and had started fanning the air with it. He said, "Smells like somethin died in here Big Jim......let's move!"

As he said that the door going into the back room flew open and Trigger came running out and said, "What in the hell is all the commotion out here?"

"Just having a little fun with Fatso," said Big Jim. "Need to talk with Pretty Boy."

"Know how to stop an elephant from charging?", said Fatso

Big Jim and Slick just looked at him. "You take away his credit card!" responded Fatso, as he relaxed back into his chair with a big grin on his large face.

"Yeah Slick, time to get out of here," said Big Jim as he and Slick followed Trigger through the back room door.

Pretty Boy sat behind his desk. Although very careful about his dress and general appearance, and demanded that the office always be kept neat and orderly, Pretty Boy had one very disgusting habit. He chewed tobacco. He loved chewing tobacco. He nearly always kept a chew in one of his cheeks, and the juice would always find its way out the corner of his mouth and down each side to his chin to form brown stained lines on both sides of his mouth. He spit into a styrofoam cup that contained tissue paper to absorb the juice.

"Well, well, well. It looks like Big Jim and Slick from Floyd County have graced my domicile," said Pretty Boy. "My bet would be this visit has something to do with the $200,000 that your driver lost when he tried to move that tree with his car."

"Marty was a good man Pretty Boy. He just made a mistake and was driving too fast. I'd appreciate it if you showed him a little respect," Big Jim responded. "But you would be right that I'm here to talk about getting that 200K back. And since you would have made 20K from that money I'm surprised you hadn't contacted me about it."

"Big Jim I figured you'd come up with something to get it back, but I never thought you'd send Slick to stick up the sheriff's office. And then the story I heard was that a pussy cat stopped him dead in his tracks." said Pretty Boy with a big grin on his tobacco stained face.

Slick turned red in the face as he reached up and rubbed around the top of his bandaged head. "That was no normal cat," said Slick

"Yeah, yeah," said Pretty Boy. "Better take a big dog with you on your next robbery!"

To which Big Jim said, "Speaking of which, I want to tell you my plan. As you know, the sheriff's office is open from 8 am to midnight. Any calls that go to the sheriffs office after midnight get transferred to the Kentucky State Police. And the sheriffs office only has one person in it from 4 pm to midnight .... guess they're on a limited budget. So what I want to do is for you to have Trigger take Slick to the sheriff's office just before midnight and park around at the back door. Deputy Bill Black will be on duty, and when he leaves he'll go out the back door to get his car in the parking lot. Trigger and Slick will stand outside the back door, one on each side. When Black comes out they knock him in the head, put a bag over his head, and tie his hands behind him, and then put him out of sight somewhere in the parking lot. Then Trigger will get back in his car and stand watch while Slick goes back in through the back door, gets the $200, 000 from the evidence room, and then back out the back door and the two of them will hightail it back here with the money. If anyone comes around while Slick is in the office Trigger can call him on his cell phone.".

"Might work," said Pretty Boy. "You better try it tonight ..... I don't know how much longer they will leave the money in the evidence room before the sheriff gets the court to let him transfer it to the county's bank account."

Big Jim got a sly smile on his face and said, "That's just what I had in mind. I'll leave Slick here with you two, and I'm headed back to Floyd County. After the job tonight work something out to get Slick a car so he can drive back home. Appreciate your help with all this."

Trigger nodded. Pretty Boy spit in his cup and said, "Watch those curves on your way home Big Jim.".

Big Jim went through the door back into the grocery store, headed for the front door and his car. As he passed through the grocery Fatso saw him and said, "Hey Big Jim, know what the elephant said to the naked man?".

Big Jim stopped, looked at Fatso, and said, "I haven't a clue."

Fatso said, "The elephant said to the naked man, I just don't see how you could possibly breathe through that little thing!"

Big Jim shook his head and left. Fatso roared.

Trigger and Slick left Maggard's grocery around 11 pm after playing poker all evening. They got to Harlan and to the sheriff's office about 30 minutes later, and parked on the street and watched to see if anyone went in. Everything was quiet. At about a quarter of midnight Trigger drove his car into the parking lot behind the sheriff's office building. Just before midnight the two got out and stationed themselves on either side of the back door. Slick had his gun out and with his right hand holding the barrel was ready to hit the deputy with the gun's handle. Trigger held a cloth bag and rope in his left hand. After about 5 minutes the back door swung open and deputy Black stepped out. Slick popped him atop his head with his gun handle, and he started falling. Trigger grabbed him with his right hand and with Slick's help they eased him to the ground and put the bag over his head and tied his hands. They then drug him beside the dumpster, and Trigger got back in his car as Slick entered the evidence room. He then started rummaging through drawers and shelves in search of the money. After a bit he came to a drawer that had what looked to be the money wrapped in saran wrap. He could see the $100 bills, and it looked to be about the right size, and then he saw the label that indicated the date and a reference number. The date corresponded. He had it!!

Just then his cell phone rang. He answered and heard Trigger say "We got company....the Harlan City Police are coming up the street slowly, I'm getting out of here. You better head out the front door, and then give me a call in about 15 minutes and I'll pick you up.". Slick said, "Fine," and slammed his cell shut and into his pocket, grabbed the large package of money, and started toward the front of the sheriff's office. He got to the front door, and then after opening the front door he held the money package under his left arm as he got his revolver out ready for anyone that might be in his path out the front door. That was a mistake.

Next thing Slick knew his world again went black and the intense pain was back in the top of his head.

A homeless person who was sitting on the front lawn of the sheriff's office just outside the front door later told the sheriff what he saw. He said he was just getting ready to lay down to sleep when the front door burst open and he saw a figure start to emerge with a package under one arm and holding a pistol in the other hand. He said he next heard terrible screams and saw the man drop the package and start to run with what looked like a grey "Davy Crockett" coon-skinned fur hat on his head, complete with a long tail that was swishing back and forth. Then the guy dropped his gun and his hat flew off. And It looked like he had a lot of blood running down his head. Then the homeless guy said, "And to top it all off, it then looked like the fur hat began to move and walked back into your office! It was then that I swore I'd never take another sip of that bay rum!"

Sheriff Sterling and Deputy Cornett had arrived after they got a call from the City Police only about 15 minutes after the incident. The City Police told the sheriff that they found the package of money laying just outside the front door, but that they only saw the homeless man and not the intruder. They said they found Deputy Black tied up in the back parking lot, unharmed except for a bad headache and cut on his head.

All the officers went in the front door and turned on the lights in the office. They looked up at the shelf by the window and door where Preacher Puss often lay, and there they saw the cat looking down at them with big yellow eyes and swishing tail. Bert reached up and gave the cat a nice stroke. Preacher Puss purred approvingly.

Trigger got a call from Slick asking that he pick him up behind the post office. Trigger circled behind the post office and saw a bloodied Slick get into the car without the money.

"And just exactly where is the money?" said Trigger

"The sheriff's got this beast that guards his office," said Slick. "He jumped me from somewhere just as I was making it out the front door with the money. Dug fangs into my head. Worst damn thing I ever felt. I dropped the money and gun and got out of Dodge. I'm not going back there. Big Jim can get somebody else for this job.".

"Yeah," said Trigger. "He probably will".

9.

The Reverend Raymond Bell was pastor of the New Hope Baptist Church in Harlan. Pastor Bell was born in Tavares, Florida. After graduating from Tavares High School he attended Florida State University in Tallahassee, and graduated with a major in history. Being a brilliant student, he was encouraged by his professors to continue his studies, and after 2 more years received his Masters Degree in history. As a child his family had vacationed frequently in Kentucky because his mother was originally from Lexington. On these vacations they traveled over the state and Raymond developed a deep love and appreciation for the Blue Grass state.

After finishing school at Florida State, Raymond married Betty, his sweetheart from high school, and they decided to move to Lexington to teach at Bryan Station High School. Raymond taught history and Betty taught art. After one year Raymond felt called to the ministry, and enrolled at Asbury Theological Seminary in nearby Wilmore, Kentucky, and received a Master of Theology Degree there three years later.

Raymond and Betty then began to search for a church, and after several visits to churches over the state decided to accept the call extended by the New Hope Baptist Church in Harlan. Both Raymond and Betty had been active in their Baptist churches in Tavares, Tallahassee, and Lexington. They were readily accepted at New Hope, and also by the people in Harlan. Everyone loved Raymond and Betty, and they loved the mountain people in Harlan.

Raymond had received a phone call from Carolyn Potter early this morning saying she and her son Kylie needed to talk with him. He told them he had just finished preparing the church service for tomorrow, and would be happy to see them. They agreed on 11 am.

Carolyn had always attended New Hope Baptist. Her parents were faithful members there, and as she grew up she always attended services at New Hope with her parents. When she was in High School she joined the church, and had been very active in several different ministries. She had known Pastor Bell since he and his wife came to New Hope, and she respected them greatly. Pastor Bell had always thought highly of Carolyn, but had serious reservations about her marriage to Snake. Snake was certainly not a believer, and even made light of Carolyn's belief on more than one occasion when Rev. Bell was present. Snake reluctantly agreed to a couple of sessions of marriage counseling when Carolyn and Snake asked Pastor Bell to conduct their wedding. But Snake always seemed less than sincere. Nevertheless, Carolyn seemed deeply in love with him and had told the pastor that she felt sure she could bring about positive changes in Snake. That didn't happen.

Carolyn and Kylie arrived at the church a few minutes before 11 am, and knocked on Pastor Bell's office door.

"Please do come in," said Pastor Bell

Carolyn walked in holding Kylie's hand. They both hugged Pastor Bell and then took a seat on the sofa across from Pastor Bell's desk.

"It is so good as always to see the two of you," said the pastor. "I hope both of you and your mother are doing well. I should hope good wishes for Snake as well, but honestly, I do think the good Lord is still working hard on him."

"Thanks Reverend Bell. Mom's fine, and we are too. Snake is Snake, but that's not why we are here today," Carolyn said. "Kylie, why don't you tell Pastor Bell the story of how you found your buried treasure."

"Hey, this sounds like it's going to be real exciting ..... buried treasure!! Let me hear about it Kylie," said the pastor.

Kylie proceeded to tell his story about hiking the river and into the woods and discovering the beautiful cross and the bones. Then Kylie reached into his pocket and carefully removed the golden cross.

Pastor Bell looked astonished!! He said, "My, my Kylie. That does indeed look like a treasure. Could I examine it?"

Kylie carefully placed it in the pastor's hands.

Pastor Bell took several minutes to carefully examine both sides of the cross as well as it's edges. Then he said, "This is just astounding. I've read about, and seen pictures of relics such as this, but certainly it's my first time to actually hold and examine one. This appears to be what is called an "Anchor Cross". Being the Christians that you two are, you well know that Christ died on a cross for our sins and was resurrected from the dead three days later. And so the cross today is a symbol everyone associates with Christ and his gift to us. What most people don't know is that the cross did not become a religious symbol until more than 300 years after his death. You see, before and after Christ's death the cross was associated with criminals. It represented the way the most despised people were put to death. It was about 325 AD that the Emperor Constantine was converted to Christianity and the cross was first used as a symbol associated with Christ.

From this time back to the death of Christ the anchor was well established as the early Christian symbol. Hebrews 6:19 says, "We have this hope as an anchor for the soul, firm and secure." Anchors were symbols on tombs back as far as the end of the first century. Even before Christ anchors were associated with faith."

Pastor Bell continued, "Combining the anchor and cross produced what is called the Anchor Cross. There were many versions of the Anchor Cross, including the St. Peter's Cross, the Admiralty pattern, The Wheel Cross, the Moline Cross, and lots of others. The common theme in all of them is the presence of both the anchor and the cross. As I examine this cross I notice that it appears to be made of purest gold, and that in addition to having the anchor and cross together it also has an inscription on the horizontal arm of the cross that says pax tecum. This is Latin, and can be translated to mean "peace be with you". I feel that this anchor cross could date back to the Roman Empire, perhaps from the 4th century. It is priceless! How it came to be buried in Harlan County may well never be known. But I feel sure that it was brought here by an early settler, and lost. I can certainly look for pictures of known early anchor crosses to see if I can locate one like this one, and I can try contacting some of my professors at Asbury and historians at FSU to see what they might have to say about it. What do you think?"

Carolyn and Kylie had looks of amazement on their faces. Carolyn then said, "I think researching it further would surely be in order. And we might also want to schedule a visit to the site where it was found. There could be some answers associated with the bones. But first I think you need to hear the rest of Kylie's story."

"Oh," replied Pastor Bell, "by all means. I'm sorry, I didn't realize there was more."

Kylie looked at his mother and said, "Mom, why don't you start this part."

Carolyn nodded, and began, "Kylie was very confused by his find, and had not told anyone for a time after he found the cross and bones. He had carefully hidden the cross in his pockets, a pants pocket during the day and a pajama pocket at night. So last night after Kylie had gone to bed Snake came home drunk," Carolyn paused, and then continued, "and started his ranting and raving and threw a few things. Kylie heard the racket and slipped downstairs. Snake and I were in the kitchen. Kylie, I think you can better tell what happened from here."

"Well, I saw dad screaming at mom. She was sitting in a kitchen chair and dad was right in front of her cussing and being mean," Kylie said. "Then he seemed to get real mad and turned red in the face and said he needed to teach her a lesson and picked up my baseball bat. He drew it back over his head, and I could sense he was going to hit mother real hard with it. I knew I had to try to stop him and ran with my arms up and jumped between them just as he brought the bat down as hard as he could. I just knew it would break my arm and possibly still hurt mom …. but I just had to try. And then what happened I can't explain or understand. Just before the bat struck my arm it seemed to hit something and bounced back and hit dad on his forehead. Dad then just slumped to the floor out cold. It was at that time that I felt something hot in my pj pocket, and reached in and pulled out the cross. That was the first time mother saw it".

"It astonished me," said Carolyn. "We left immediately for my mother's house and spent the night there, and called you this morning. My guess is that Snake is still sleeping it off on the kitchen floor."

Pastor Bell nodded slowly as he continued his inspection of the cross. Then he said, "That truly is amazing. I don't have an explanation, either about the bat encountering something invisible or about the heat you felt from the cross. I'll add these facts to the story that I relate to my professors and researchers and get their take on it. What I do know, however, is that your experience with the anchor cross was one that reinforced the inscribed pax tecum, or "peace be with you". I know it is all very confusing to both of you, and my best advice right now would be to go back to Mawie's house and spend the rest of the weekend there to avoid Snake and let him sober up. I'll see you all at church tomorrow, and when I have news from my contacts about the cross I'll be in touch. In the meantime, maybe one afternoon next week after school and work we could meet and take a look at the place where Kylie found the cross."

Carolyn and Kylie thanked and hugged Pastor Bell and said they agreed with his suggestions, and then left for Mawies.

10.

It was Monday morning. Bad Eye had just called a meeting with Snake, Jones Anderson, and Billie Lingal.

Bad Eye told everyone to be seated. The only desk at the junk yard was one that someone had discarded about 10 years ago, and Bad Eye set it up in a corner of the one-room junk yard office building. The rest of the room was piled high with years of collected junk, and there was a smelly restroom in the corner opposite that which contained Bad Eye's desk.

The boys gathered some folding chairs and sat in front of the desk.

"Bet the time has come that we're going to hear about your big retirement plan," Snake said.

Bad Eye looked at Snake and said, "That's what I had in mind, but from the looks of that knot and bruise on your head I don't know if you're going to be up to doing anything Snake."

"Just a scratch, Bad Eye. I somehow got hit in the head during an argument with the wife. I was a bit under the 'shine at the time, and don't remember much about how it happened. I do know it took me till this morning to get rid of a splitting headache, but I'll be fine. Just makes me more interested in retiring. Lets hear the plan."

Jones & Billie nodded.

Bad Eye fired up another cigar, then leaned back in his chair and began talking, "Well, like I said when we talked last time, if you want money it seems to me like you go to a bank. The bank I've got in mind is the Harlan Miners Bank. Now what you guys might not know is that most banks really don't have a lot of cash on hand. True, they get deposits and they keep plenty to pay out ..... but short of some unusual situation they might not have more than several thousand in cash on hand at any one time. Can't retire on a few thousand. So I've done a little poking around to see if there might be a time when we could hit them when they had several million. That's more like the retirement I had in mind."

Bad Eye looked at each of the three to gauge their response, and decided they looked about as interested as they were capable of looking. So he took another big puff on the cigar and blew a cloud of smoke out over his desk and continued, "Now you know you ain't suppose to say anything at all about what I getting ready to tell you, and if I find out you have blabbed it you'll pay dearly. Here's the deal. I know you all know Julie Lacey who works at Miners Bank. Snake, I know you know her especially since Carolyn is also a teller there and she and Carolyn work together."

"I know her," said Snake. "She and the old lady do both work there, but Carolyn has never really liked Julie. The two sort of run in different circles, if you follow me. Julie is young and single and likes to party and all that, and Carolyn's not into that stuff. They just kind of coexist at the bank ...... they're not close."

"Don't matter," said Bad Eye. "Julie's the one that's important to us. I was at a party a few weeks back and Julie and I got to talking and drinking and drinking and talking, and before I knew it we were the only ones left. Everyone else had gone home. She was blabbing on about everything that came into her inebriated mind, and we started talking about how we both would like to take a grand around-the-world cruise, but couldn't because we didn't have the money. She then said something like "well if I had just a little of the money that's in Pretty Boy's lock boxes we could go around the world and then on to the moon and back". I was pretty sauced, but when she came out with that I sobered up pretty fast."

Bad Eye had their attention now. Each of the three had their mouth slightly open, a smile on their face, and an eager look. He continued, "So I said what kind of money does Pretty Boy keep in his lock box? She said, "Not one lock box ...... he's got two of the real big ones." So I asked why he had two, and she said he accumulated cash in them for about three months and then took it all out and started over again. She said she had seen the bundles of cash that went into the lock boxes, and they looked like mostly one hundred dollar bills. So I asked when he took the money out, and she said the first work day of each quarter he would come by with Trigger and the two of them would go in the vault with a couple of large bags and remove the cash. I asked her if that didn't look a little strange to everyone at the bank and she said they always arrived during lunch and she and Carolyn were usually the only ones there and that Carolyn was always busy at a tellers window while she looked after the vault and safe deposit boxes. She said Pretty Boy would always arrive first and go into the vault and start filling his bag, and then Trigger would show up and go into the vault with Pretty Boy, and then the two of them would leave about five minutes apart, each with a big bag of cash. And once every three months didn't raise suspicion."

Snake got a funny look on his face and said, "Bad Eye, you ain't planning on hitting Pretty Boy and Trigger are you?"

"No, no, no", said Bad Eye, "That could get real nasty. I figure it would be much easier to get their money from the bank. What I've got in mind is to get all their money, all that the bank has, and all that's in the other safe deposit boxes too."

"And exactly how you think we might pull that off?", said Snake.

"Just before she passed out dead drunk I asked Julie about how anyone might be able to open the safe deposit boxes," Bad Eye continued. "It was a bit slurred, but what I understood was that for a whole variety of reasons the bank had to have the ability to open a safe deposit box without having the owners key. The bank has one very special pass key that can be used to open a safe deposit box without the use of the box owners key. There was only one such pass key and it was kept in the desk of the bank president Calvin Brown. If someone died and their heirs could not find their safe deposit box key, for example, then Calvin Brown would go in the vault usually with an attorney from the estate of the deceased and open the box with the pass key. At other times people just lost their key, and the same procedure would be used, and always with an expensive fee paid to the bank."

Snake, Jones, and Billie all nodded quickly with a great smile.

"So," said Bad Eye, "all we got to do is get that pass key, put our plan together, and our retirement awaits us!"

"You think Julie remembers any of your conversation?" asked Snake.

"Not a chance. She was drunk as a skunk," replied Bad Eye. "So now you know what I've got in mind for our retirement. Anyone see any problem?".

Snake, Jones, and Billie all looked at each other, and then Snake said, "Bad Eye, that sounds like a plan to me. All we need to do is work out the details of the hit. I think I'll go ahead and start making retirement plans! When do we do it?".

"The last day of this quarter is coming up in about two weeks," Bad Eye replied. "I think we can put our plan together by then, and be retired by the first of next month!".

All four smiled and nodded in agreement, and Bad Eye blew another big cloud of smoke over his desk. Jones and Billie high-fived each other. Snake reached up and rubbed his sore head.

11.

After Carolyn and Kylie left Saturday morning, Pastor Bell was so excited about Kylie's story and about the beautiful golden anchor cross that he just could not stop thinking about them. If in fact the cross did date back to the 4th Century after Christ it was certainly a very historic as well as religious find. And to think that just moments ago he actually held the cross in his very hands. And it was found in Harlan County!

Since he really couldn't get his mind off it, Pastor Bell started to consider several of his old professors and acquaintances thinking about the need to contact someone to get additional information about the cross. He thought about several active historical researchers he knew from Florida State and Asbury, but then he realized that the perfect contact would be Dr. Randy Peters who headed up the Center for Appalachian Research at the University of Kentucky. Raymond had become good friends with Randy while living in Lexington. They first met when he attended a seminar entitled "The History of Harlan County" that Dr. Peters conducted. Raymond had noticed an announcement in the Lexington newspaper, the Herald-Leader, and because of his love of Kentucky and history he decided to attend. As it turned out, Randy

Peters' doctorial dissertation concerned the history of Harlan County, and he was certainly among the most highly qualified and knowledgeable authorities on the subject. After the seminar Raymond approached Randy expressing how much he enjoyed the seminar, and after another 15 minutes of chit-chat the two became good friends and frequently got together for lunch or dinner.

So Pastor Raymond Bell gave Dr. Randy Peters a call that hopefully would help Raymond understand more about the cross and how it happened into Harlan County.

"Hey Raymond, how good to hear from you," said Randy Peters. "I was beginning to think you had gotten all settled there in God's country and forgotten all about your old buddy here in Lexington!"

Raymond was so glad to hear Randy's voice. It was largely because of him that he and Betty had decided to accept the call to pastor New Hope Baptist in Harlan. Randy constantly talked about Harlan, and always in glowing terms. So when the call from New Hope was extended, Raymond felt that Harlan was certainly where the Lord intended him to go.

"I could never forget such a great friend," said Raymond. "Just been busy .... too busy perhaps. And that's really no excuse. You'll just have to pardon my failure to keep in touch as often as I should, but believe me you are remembered fondly by me very frequently. How's everything going at the CAR?" Raymond referring to the Center for Appalachian Research.

Randy responded, "Well, you know academia. Ups and downs. But generally things seem to be going smoothly ..... at least as far as I know! I bet you might have a question."

"You always did have a crystal ball! I certainly did want to touch base with you, but I must admit that, as usual, you are correct. I do indeed have a question. In fact, I have several of them, and they all have to do with Harlan County history."

"You made the right call Raymond," responded Randy. "I do know a bit about it, and certainly am most anxious to be of help to my good friend. So what's up?"

Raymond told Kylie's story to Randy. He told Randy that he had told Carolyn and Kylie that he would do his best to get further information and would also try and maintain confidentiality so that if Kylie's find was as valuable as Raymond thought it might be, their identity would be protected.   Raymond was thinking about all the media attention that could result, and even the possibility of someone attempting to rob the Potters of the cross, so he thought it best to try and keep the story out of the public for the time being.

After hearing the story, there was a long pause on the telephone. Raymond thought he might have lost connection, and said, "Randy, you there?"

"Sorry Raymond, I was just thinking. That story is astounding. As soon as you mentioned the golden anchor cross a big light went on in my brain. I certainly don't know if it is the same one, but I recall a long, detailed entry into the diary of Samuel Howard, the founder of Harlan County, that talked at length about a golden anchor cross. I'll have to dig into my archives to find the diary and read again about it before I can really tell you anything else, but my intuition tells me we really might have something here. Can I get back with you shortly?"

"Of course, my friend. I truly appreciate you, and will look forward greatly to your call. Thanks again .... good bye," and Pastor Bell immediately started looking forward to Randy's return call.

12.

Sheriff J. Bert Sterling had seen lots of changes in the Harlan County Sheriff's office during his time there, which now totaled 30 years, the first 15 as a deputy and the last 15 as sheriff. Harlan County's population was definitely on the decrease. When it was founded in 1820 there were 1,961 persons in the County. Population started to grow, and by 1940 it had risen to 75, 275. And then it began it's decline. The 2010 census showed a decrease to 29,278. There was little manufacturing and limited small farms. Coal was still king, but it was being mined with automated equipment that required fewer and fewer miners. The two largest sources of revenue in the country were coal and government checks. And the outlook was not good. So with a decreasing tax base, the Sheriff's office had struggled to maintain adequate personnel and equipment to properly serve and protect the citizens of the county. Bert was always applying for grants from various agencies to supplement the office's budget, but such funds were sought by many applicants and difficult to secure.

Currently the sheriff's office had only 6 employees out of the Harlan office, and an additional 5 that operated out of a satellite office in Cumberland, about 25 miles

Northeast of Harlan on highway 119. Both offices had limited their hours to 8 am to midnight, which meant there were two shifts, one from 8 am to 4:30 pm, and the second from 4:30 pm to midnight. From Midnight to 8 am calls that went to the sheriff's office were directed to the Kentucky State Police. Post 10 was headquartered just East of downtown Harlan. This arrangement, although not ideal, was working adequately.

Personnel at the Harlan sheriff's office, in addition to Sheriff Sterling, included Ape Cornett, Rosie Cain, Simpson Brown, Mousy Giles, and Bill Black. The Sheriff, Ape, Rosie, and Simpson normally worked the first shift, and Mousy and Bill the second. For the second shift Bill normally worked in the office, and Mousy made rounds and responded to calls in a patrol car.

It was a quiet day, and Bert and Ape decided to take a mid morning coffee break at Creech Cafe, which was located just across Central Street from the sheriff's office.

As Bert and Ape walked in the door the owner, Fred Knapp, warmly greeted them, "Top of the morning guys .... hope all is running well in the sheriff's office"

"Morning Fred," Bert and Ape each said and then took a stool at the counter.

Creech Cafe was a landmark in Harlan. It had been operated by Fred Knapp for over 40 years. Fred had started working in the cafe for his father while going to Harlan High School, and to the delight of his dad had decided to make a career there. Kids stopped in after school each day, and regulars gathered daily to meet, greet, eat, and solve world problems. Creech's was the most popular cafe in town, and all that went there loved Fred.

Polly had been with Fred for about 10 years. She was a large, green parrot, and always positioned herself on a rod that Fred had mounted next to the door. Polly had a pretty good vocabulary, and she recognized most of the regulars that came into the cafe each day with a, "Polly want a cracker, Polly want a cracker". Often times she would be rewarded with some bit of food reached up to her bill. After grabbing the food and eating it she would then usually say, "Polly thanks. Polly thanks". The patrons in the cafe always enjoyed seeing and listening to Polly. About three years back there was quite a stir in town when someone reported Polly as violating some vague sanitary regulation, but when the case came up in court there was such an outpouring of support for Polly that the judge dismissed the charges and all returned to normal at Creechs.

The most popular story about Polly, and one known by most everyone in Harlan County, happened 5 years ago. Polly's owner, Fred Knapp, lives alone in a large, older home on Mound Street. Polly usually stayed in the store during the week, but Fred didn't work on Saturday and the store was closed on Sunday so he always would bring Polly home for the weekend. Because there had been a break-in at a home 3 doors down from Fred earlier that year, Fred decided he would get a pit bull dog to guard his home. He also decided to install a security system that had several cameras positioned in various locations in and outside his home. A few months later Fred had traveled to Pineville on a Saturday to visit friends. While he was gone a burglar struck Fred's home. All the details of what happened during that burglary were captured on video tape from the security cameras. It was later a lead story on the front page of the Harlan Daily Enterprise, as follows:

BURGLARY ATTEMPT AT FRED KNAPP'S HOME
ABORTED BY PARROT AND DOG

Last Saturday afternoon a burglar broke into the home of Creech Cafe owner Fred Knapp. The attempted robbery was caught on several security cameras in Knapp's home, and revealed the following. After gaining entry through the back door the robber moved to the basement to start searching for items of interest. He was carrying a large duffel bag into which he apparently was going to place the stolen items. Once into the dimly lit basement he encountered Knapp's parrot Polly, well known to all who frequent Creech Cafe. Polly had positioned herself atop the back of a wooden chair and as soon as she saw the burglar she started saying, "Polly want a cracker, Polly want a cracker, Polly want a cracker". It appeared to scare the burglar at first, and then he screamed to Polly, "Shut the f--- up, you damn dumb bird!". To which Polly responded, "Polly want a cracker, Polly want a cracker, Polly want a cracker". At this point the robber glanced over into a dark corner of the room and saw Brutus, Knapp's huge, vicious pit bull dog. Brutus was just sitting, looking intently at the robber. When the robber saw the dog he froze and was obviously greatly frightened. Then he said to the dog, "Good doggie, good doggie," and then spoke softly to himself, "That dog hasn't moved, and looks like I might get away without him bothering me .... so I'll continue.". Polly continued saying, "Polly want a cracker, Polly want a cracker, Polly want a cracker." The robber went through Knapps desk and several cabinets removing valuables and placing them in his duffel bag. Finally he finished, and as he was *starting to go up the stairs Polly again repeated, "Polly want a cracker, Polly want a cracker, Polly want a cracker.". The robber stopped and looked at the bird and just couldn't resist saying to Polly, "Can't you say anything but Polly want a cracker?". At that point the camera seemed to show a slight grin on Polly's beak, and then she said, "Sic 'em!".*

The end of the attempted robbery was caught by an outside surveillance camera. The front door to Knapp's home flew open and the burglar came flying out with Brutus firmly attached to his rear end. Brutus fell to the ground with what appeared to be a large chunk of flesh and the better part of the seat of the burglar's trousers. The burglar dropped his duffel bag as he increased his speed down Mound Street. Neighbors called 911, and after the police arrived they found the duffel bag and the large piece of flesh attached to a piece of cloth. They are investigating to identify the burglar.

Fred liked to frame and put photographs up on the walls at Creech Cafe. There was one that had the above Enterprise article, and beside it in a frame was a piece of dark, discolored flesh attached to a piece of cloth that were both enclosed in a zip-locked bag. Fred always liked to say about these prizes, "We never did catch that burglar, but Brutus sure got a good piece of his ass!"

"You boys having breakfast or just coffee?" Fred asked Bert and Ape.

"Just coffee this morning, Fred, got to get back to the office and try and catch some crooks." Bert said.

Fred nodded and poured hot, steaming coffee into two mugs.

13.

Fatso was bent over, restocking groceries on a bottom shelf at Maggard's grocery. Big Jim walked in unnoticed and saw Fatso all bent over and went over and slapped him on the rear.

Fatso jumped, and in doing so he cracked the back of his head on one of the upper shelves. "Dad burn you Big Jim, every time you come in here you cause me trouble!"

Big Jim said, "Fatso, I am sorry. I didn't really intend to cause you to whack your head. Please forgive me."

Fatso said, "Well, I guess I can do that."

Big Jim said, "Fatso, I've been thinking that it is just not politically correct to call you Fatso. So in the future I'm not going to do that"

Fatso said, "O.K., but everyone calls me Fatso, and I've sort of gotten used to it. But that's mighty big of you to think about me that way." And Fatso walked back behind the counter to push the button to allow Big Jim entry into the back room.

"Thanks," said Big Jim as he opened the back room door, and as he started in he added, "I appreciate that Lard Ass!" and slammed the door behind him.

Pretty Boy looked up from his desk with a grin on his tobacco streaked chin.

Trigger turned from his computer desk to look at Big Jim and said, "Can't you close the door a little quieter?"

"Howdy boys," said Big Jim. "Good to see the two of you. I wanted to personally bring you this delivery, since I haven't been having much luck in that department lately." And he placed a bag on Pretty Boy's desk.

"You can count it later Pretty Boy, but you'll find about $175K in there. I had the good fortune for one of my clients to ante up a payment he owed me and I thought since that last one got appropriated by the good Harlan County sheriff I'd just mosey down here myself with this one to make sure it got credited to my account."

"Your business is booming up there in Floyd County Big Jim," said Pretty Boy. "I am truly sorry about Marty losing that 200K for you. And I know you heard that the sheriff finally got the court to let him transfer the money from his office into the county's bank account. So there went any chance you still had to get it back. But from what I heard Slick really didn't want to try again anyway, what with that mean ole pussy cat guarding the money!" Pretty Boy giggled as he spit tobacco juice into his Styrofoam cup.

"I still don't know what to believe about those stories," said Big Jim. "Slick has always been faithful, but something really got to him on those two botched jobs. But, like you say, that's water over the dam now, so just got to move on."

"Yep, that's the way I figure it," said Pretty Boy patting Big Jim's money bag on his desk. "Trigger, you need to call Julie at the bank and set up another deposit. We can't leave this money sitting around here. You just never know when ole sheriff Sterling might up and decide to pay us a visit."

"I'm on it," said Trigger as he grabbed the bag and slapped his cell phone to his ear.

Big Jim and Trigger walked out the door into the grocery store together, and as they passed through the grocery store Big Jim looked over at Fatso and said, "Later, Lard Ass."

Fatso said, "Know why the Elephant crossed the road Big Jim?"

Big Jim just shook his head as Fatso said, "Because it was the chicken's day off."

"I'll go back to calling you Fatso if you'll stop with those stupid jokes," said Big Jim, and out the front door he went with Trigger.

14.

Dr. Randy Peters called Pastor Raymond Bell late on Monday afternoon.

"Hey Raymond, Randy here getting back to you with information about the cross."

"Randy, you just don't know how good it is to hear your voice. Since we talked last Saturday I've hardly been able to think about anything else. This is the most exciting thing I've encountered in a long, long time," said Pastor Bell.

Randy responded, "Yeah, I hear you. It's been the same for me, so I started to dig into the archives soon after our conversation. The mention of that beautiful golden cross really hit a cord with me .... I just felt sure there was mention of such in the diary of Samuel Howard."

"So did you find it?" said Raymond.

"Sure did," said Randy. "Samuel Howard was not only the first settler in what is now Harlan, but he was also extremely meticulous in keeping a detailed diary of his activities. I'm sure he realized the importance of being the first settler in the area, and likely knew that future generations would want to know details of his adventures."

Pastor Bell replied, "And he was correct .... here we are some 200 plus years later searching for just that."

"True," said Randy. "and I think we have it! As it turns out, Samuel Howard had met a pastor by the name of Karl Seibert while the two of them lived in Williamsburg, Virginia. They first met in 1792. Seibert had immigrated from Germany and was living and working with another pastor friend in Williamsburg. Howard and Seibert became close friends. Samuel Howard shared with Karl his vision to travel to Appalachia and to start a new life there. Howard then fulfilled his vision in 1796 when he left Williamsburg and followed the Wilderness Trail, blazed by Daniel Boone in 1775, through Cumberland Gap and then turned Northeast following the Cumberland River for about 30 miles to establish the settlement he called Mount Pleasant, later named Harlan in honor of Revolutionary War hero Silas Harlan. Major Silas Harlan served under General George Washington, and died fighting Indians at the Battle of Blue Licks near Lexington, Kentucky."

"Fascinating," commented Pastor Bell. "Please continue."

"Well, in the mean time it appears Karl Seibert met and married his wife whose name was Mary. And this occurred in 1798, and was mentioned in Howard's diary by saying he had received a letter from Karl describing in detail his meeting her, their courtship, and marriage. Incidentally, the U.S. postal service did exist at this early date. The second Continental Congress in 1775 appointed Benjamin Franklin as our first Postmaster General. Naturally the mail service was greatly slower than today, but letters did eventually get through. Anyway, Karl had received a request from Samuel Howard prior to the marriage requesting him to consider coming to Mount Pleasant to start a church. So after marrying Mary and with her consent, the two made preparations to leave with a wagon train going West. Their marriage was early in 1798, and they left for Mount Pleasant just a few months later."

"And I bet you're getting ready to tell me about the golden cross," said Pastor Bell.

"Just getting around to that," said Randy. "In his diary, Samuel Howard wrote the following passage."

In a letter received today from my good friend Karl Seibert in Williamsburg, he announced, to my great joy, that he and his new wife Mary were going to follow his Lord's direction to come to Mount Pleasant to start a church. In his letter he indicated that he had prayed at length about this decision, and that during one of these prayers he felt his chest getting very warm, and reached down and grabbed a golden anchor cross that hung about his neck. He said the cross was quite warm, and when he held it he immediately saw a vision that affirmed that he should make the journey. This was the same golden anchor cross that Karl had shown me and talked about when we were in Williamsburg together. There he told me a story about how the cross had somehow saved his life in a fall from a high cliff, and that the cross had been passed down through the Seibert family for generations. In his letter he indicated that he felt that he and Mary would be kept safe during his journey to Mount Pleasant because of his wearing the cross. I do recall how very beautiful the cross was, and I recall while examining it I found the words pax tecum inscribed on the horizontal arm of the cross. I look forward with great excitement to the arrival of Karl and Mary.

"The diary entry was dated July 10th, 1798," said Randy.

"Wow," said Raymond. "That's almost spooky. It sure does seem to describe exactly the cross that Kylie found. And it explains some of the ruins around the area where he found the cross. I bet when we search that area we'll find the bones of Karl and Mary and other remnants from their wagon."

"My thoughts as well," said Randy. "And because of my intense interest, I was going to ask if you thought maybe Carolyn and Kylie Potter would allow me to come to Harlan and be with you when you go to look at the site."

Raymond replied, "Randy I think they would be honored to have you there. You have been so helpful, and with your background on both the history of Harlan County and your knowledge of the Seibert trip from studying the diary of Samuel Howard I know that your presence would aid us to sift through the site looking for anything that could shed light on Kylie's find. When could you come to Harlan?"

"I know everyone is excited about all this," said Randy. "So I would like to make the trip Wednesday, if that is agreeable. I could meet you at your church around 3 pm, and then we could drive to Wallins and meet Carolyn and Kylie at Carolyn's mom's house and leave from there hiking to the site. It doesn't get dark until later, so we should have plenty of time to look, at least to make a first pass. If need be we could schedule a second trip later. Does that sound o.k. to you?"

"Sounds fine to me Randy .... see you Wednesday around 3 at the church."

15.

Sheriff J. Bert Sterling was sitting in his office, feet up on his desk, talking to Deputy Ape Cornett, "I'm just getting bad vibrations about the money that turned up in that car wreck, and the two attempts to get it back. If we hadn't gotten lucky with Preacher Puss, the money would now be long gone to wherever it was going. And I sure don't know for sure that it was headed somewhere here in Harlan County, but I don't know it wasn't either. I just have a bad feeling about it. What's your take on it Ape?"

"Were you able to find out where the driver was from that was killed in the wreck?" said Ape.

"Yeah, he was from Prestonsburg, up in Floyd County. He apparently worked for Big Jim Owens, the Floyd County drug dealer. And we learned that the robber we held overnight also lived up there and worked for Owens. But that's about all we know, and it's certainly not enough to charge him with anything. He's got a real slick lawyer, the guy that got the robber released, and it'd be a waste of our time and money to try and go after him just on what we now have. But I've just got this suspicion that the money from the wreck might just be the tip of the iceberg. There could be a ton of illegal money flowing into Harlan. I just don't know where it all might be coming from, where its going, and what's happening to it. Far more questions than answers."

Ape thought about what the sheriff had said, and added, "What we do know for sure is that the $200,000 that came from Floyd County is now safely residing in the Harlan County bank account. You got any ideas about other illegal monies flowing into our county?"

"Think about that all the time, Ape," said Bert. "That much money represents some real potential for bad things to happen. And we don't need any of that. I can't help but think that Pretty Boy Maggard is likely involved in all this somehow .... but I can't prove it. Every time we've raided him he's been clean. I wish we could watch him closer, but we just don't have the manpower to devote to him. I keep hoping he'll slip up, but so far it hasn't happened."

Ape nodded.

"Then there's that bunch at Bad Eye's Junkyard. Everyone knows that they are always up to no good, but I don't think they have enough sense to be involved in any kind of operation that would involve the kind of money we're talking about. We know they buy and sell stolen car parts and likely have a moonshine operation going, but we haven't even been able to bust them for any of that. They are good at what they do. I just don't think they could be involved in any kind of big money operation. So that gets us back to Pretty Boy, unless someone else has moved into Harlan that we don't know about."

"Is there anything we can do to further check-out Pretty Boy?" said Ape.

"I've been thinking about that. If he is receiving large amounts of money he has to be putting it somewhere. We pretty much know he's not keeping it at the grocery, and I'll bet he's not burying it.   So I keep wondering if he's putting it in the bank. I think maybe I'll do a little checking to see what we might be able to find out about his banking. We could get a lead there." said Bert.

"Sounds worth a try," Ape replied.

Late that afternoon Ape had walked across the street to Creech Cafe for a snack. He was seated at a table enjoying a double cheeseburger with all the trimmings.

"Polly want a cracker, Polly want a cracker, Polly want a cracker," Polly cackled from her perch beside the front door.

Ape reached down and pulled a piece of lettuce from his cheeseburger and held it high in the air. Polly immediately left her perch and flew to Ape, picking the lettuce from his fingers before landing on the top of a chair beside Ape. "Polly thanks, Polly thanks," the bird said.

"You're welcome Miss Polly," said Ape, as he continued to eat his burger.

Sheriff Sterling walked in the door, saw Ape, and walked over and joined him.

"See you been feeding Polly again," Bert said.

"Just a bit of lettuce," Ape replied. "What's new?"

"Been visiting banks," said the sheriff as Polly flew back to her perch beside the door.

"Find out anything interesting," asked Ape.

"I'm not sure," Bert replied. "But I did get some information. I visited all three of our banks, Harlan

First, City National, and Harlan Miners. Talked with the president at each bank. I had to be a bit careful what I said, because we really don't have anything specific on Pretty Boy, so I told each of them that I was just interested in seeing if he had accounts at their banks and if so could they share with me if his accounts looked unusual. I also added that our conversation was strictly confidential, and if they elected to share the information with me, which they certainly didn't have to do, then I would not disclose that they had done so outside police circles. Each of the presidents were very cooperative, and said they would be glad to assist. I found out that Pretty Boy had checking and savings accounts at Harlan First, had no accounts at City National, and had two large lock-boxes at Harlan Miners Bank."

"Hey, two large lock-boxes ..... think that might be where he stashes the cash?" asked Ape.

"That was my first thought as well, Ape, so I asked Calvin Brown, Miner's President, if he had any idea why Mr. Maggard might have two large lock-boxes. He replied that he really did not know, but he was aware that Maggard only visited his bank about once every three months or so."

Ape said, "Yeah, that looks like maybe the boxes aren't where his cash is going.....he'd have to be making lots more deposits than one every three months or so. Wouldn't you think?"

"That was exactly my thought," the sheriff said. "But it still doesn't answer the question of why he would have two large boxes there. Course he could be storing anything in them, and we certainly have no probable cause to search them. But that's the only thing of interest I could turn up in talking to the bankers. His checking and saving accounts at Harlan First Bank didn't show anything unusual.

"Guess we just keep the boxes in the back of our minds for future reference. We might be able to link them to something," Bert said.

Creech Cafe's proprietor Fred Knapp walked by the table where the sheriff and deputy sat, and said, "You two running a little late today for coffee break."

"Ape had to feed his face," said the sheriff. "And I just dropped by to rest a few minutes."

"Can I get you anything Bert" asked Fred.

"Not hungry or thirsty," said Bert as he looked up at a picture Fred had framed on the wall behind Ape. There were probably 100 framed pictures on the wall, but Bert's eye was caught by one in particular. "Hey Fred, that picture there," as he pointed, "looks like 50 or more kids in line outside a theater ..... what's the story behind that?" Bert knew Fred loved to tell stories about his walled photographs.

Fred grabbed a chair at the table with Bert and Ape and sat. "Well now, there is an interesting story behind that one," said Fred.

"Somehow I figured there would be," said Ape, as he and Bert got a big grin on their faces.

Fred continued, "That picture was taken from the court house lawn. Right across the lawn at the corner of Central and 2nd Streets used to be the Margie Grand Theater. In those days there were two movies in Harlan, the other one was the New Harlan Theater located on Main Street. What you see in that picture is indeed a line of kids waiting to get into the theater to see a Saturday cartoon show that was commonly referred to as the "Fifteen Cartoons". Once every couple of months a dairy that used to be here in Harlan called Chappell's Dairy sponsored the "Fifteen Cartoons" show by allowing kids admittance by bringing 10 tops that had been cut from their milk cartons. Back then the milk was sold mainly by the quart. Not like today when it's almost always sold by the gallon. So the kids would just take a knife and wack off the top of the quart milk carton and save up 10 of those to get into the cartoon show. If you look closely at the picture you can see that each kid is carrying a brown paper bag that contains those milk carton tops."

Bert said, "Bet that was a rowdy bunch in the theater!"

"You got that right," Fred said. "The theater was always packed. There was a balcony in the back of the theater above the main floor, and kids always filled every seat for those Fifteen Cartoon shows. Every kid in there was screaming at the top of his or her lungs, trying to talk to their friends seated beside them. The theater usually had to stop admitting kids when all the seats were full."

"Hope the fire marshal wasn't around," commented Ape.

Fred continued, "Before the show started it got so loud you really couldn't hear anything except the roar of the crowd. The show started up at 10 am. When the lights started to dim, the roar increased even more. And it was usually at least 5 minutes into the first cartoon, usually either a "Road Runner" or a "Bugs Bunny", until the noise reduced enough that you could hear the cartoon. It was really quite a happening. As a kid I attended many of those great Fifteen Cartoon shows."

Bert and Ape both nodded at Fred, and Bert said, "Good story Fred. I didn't know about those cartoon shows .... I bet the kids really enjoyed them."

"Sure did," said Fred. "I certainly have very fond memories of that old theater. When I was a kid my father used to take me every Friday evening to see a movie, and they always had what was called a serial that was shown after the movie. The movies were usually cowboys like Hopalong Cassidy, Lash LaRue, Roy Rogers, or Gene Autry. The serials were titles like "Rocket Man" or "Red Rider & Little Beaver". They were short.....not more than maybe 10 minutes long and always finished up with the hero in some precarious, impossible situation.....but he always survived, as shown the following week. I truly enjoyed those Friday evenings with my dad, and I think he even enjoyed them too."

Fred Continued, "The New Harlan Theatre was on Main Street, on the right as you headed South, just after you crossed Clover Street. One of the things I recall best about the New Harlan was they had super hot dogs ..... I think they had a special chili recipe. Man, they were good!".

Fred, Bert, and Ape all smiled and slowly nodded their head.

The Sheriff and his deputy stood up and walked over to the counter with Fred. Ape paid Fred for his snack, and as the two started out the door Polly announced, "Polly say Bye Bye, Polly say Bye Bye."

16.

Bad Eye had just sat down at his desk after asking Snake to come in to talk. Bad Eye picked up a cigar he had been puffing on for a couple of hours, and refired it up.

"What's up?" Snake asked.

"Got something I've got to ask you, and I kinda feel bad having to, but, I gotta do what I gotta do, you know?" said Bad Eye as he peered at Snake through his one good eye, and blew a small cloud of smoke over his desk.

"Sounds serious, Bad Eye," Snake answered. "Go right ahead and ask away."

"Well, as you might guess, it has to do with our retirement plans," said Bad Eye. "I been doing a lot of thinking about exactly how we going to rob that bank. The robbing part of it doesn't bother me .... I think I've got that part pretty well figured out. The part that causing me problems is how we keep the bank employees from ratting us out after the job's over .... know what I mean?"

"I think I follow you," Snake replied. "How you figure that's going to work?"

"I've thought and thought about it," said Bad Eye. "And I keep coming to the same conclusion. Everyone in that bank knows the four of us. We could try to disguise ourselves, but I just don't think we'd be successful. They'd hear our voices, and they'd see our size and mannerisms ..... I just don't think we could keep them from identifying us. Maybe they would not immediately be able to know who all four of us were, but soon as they recognized one they would likely quickly figure out the rest. So, after lots and lots of thinking, I've come to the hard conclusion that we have to do them in. That's just the only answer I come up with to be sure that they don't identify us. Even if we got away and out of the country, if they figured out who we were they'd find some way to come after us. And there would go the retirement! So the only way is to quiet them permanently. I don't feel that bad about doing it to the head man, old Calvin Brown. And Julie Lacey is just an airhead .... no big loss there. And I know Gut Blankenship will be the security guard on duty, and we'd have to do him .... no problem. But your ole lady, Carolyn, is going to be there too, and I just can't figure a way around her. I thought about some way to have her stay home, or something, but I think that would raise suspicion and could blow the whole thing. I keep coming back to the same conclusion. I think we're going to have to eliminate all four. Could you live with that, Snake?"

Snake considered what Bad Eye was proposing, and after thinking about it for a bit he started to nod his head slowly in agreement, and added, "I see your point. We never did get along that good no how. I'm thinking with all the money I'd have I could likely get me a brand spanking new one over there in the Bahamas, and maybe even one that appreciated me a lot more that Carolyn. But one things bothering me Bad Eye. After it's over and we've vamoosed, people are certainly going to notice the four of us being gone. Ain't that going to put 'em on us?"

Bad Eye grinned, blew some more smoke, and said, "I thought of that too. About a week before the bank job I'll announce the closing of the Junk Yard, and then all four of us can make known to folks that know us that we've had it here in Harlan and we've decided to head down to Knoxville to look for work. Then we'll lay low here at the Junk Yard. I'll close it up good and tight, and we'll put in supplies to get us through for a week. Should then be nothing to associate us with the bank job."

"Got to hand it to you Bad Eye, I think it just might put us all on easy street," said Snake.

When you going to tell Jones and Billie?"

"I'm still working on some of the details. Just as soon as I get everything thought out I'll get us all together and lay out the full plans," Bad Eye said. "I feel a lot better knowing your position on what we have to do ..... I was worried about that."

Snake grinned and said, "Well, like you said, you got to do what you got to do. And we all want that big payday and retirement package!"

Bad Eye nodded, took a big puff on the cigar butt, and allowed a big grin to form on his face.

17

Dr. Randy Peters parked his car in the New Hope Baptist Church parking lot after the 3 hour drive to Harlan from Lexington. Much of the road he drove on his trip overlapped the old Wilderness Trail that the early settlers had taken when traveling West after passing through Cumberland Gap. Randy entered the church and knocked on the office door of his friend Pastor Raymond Bell. It was just a few minutes before 3 pm.

"Come in, come in," Pastor Bell shouted. "I've been anxiously awaiting your arrival."

The two friends hugged, exchanged pleasantries, and then each took a seat.

Raymond said, "Randy, we've got just a few minutes before we should leave to meet Carolyn and Kylie, so I thought we could chat a bit more about this before we met them. One thing that we didn't talk much about over the phone was the mysterious occurrences that seem to befall those that have possession of the golden anchor cross. I realize that this sort of thing might well fall more into my bailiwick than yours, but I wanted to get your take on it. From what you told me, Reverend Seibert revealed two such occurrences to his friend Samuel Howard, and these got recorded in Howard's diary. The first instance related to Seibert's fall off a cliff and the second to a vision he experienced that led to his trip to Mount Pleasant, is that correct?"

"That is exactly correct, Raymond," said Randy. "I don't recall any other diary entries that addressed additional events such as those."

Raymond continued, "And then there was the thing that happened when Kylie attempted to protect his mother, and the baseball bat blow that was being delivered by Snake somehow got deflected and knocked Snake unconscious. As far as I know, these three events are associated somehow with the golden anchor cross."

"That's true," said Randy. "And we also know that Rev. Seibert said that he had heard stories from his father and grandfather in Germany that also described events that were unexplainable, but we didn't get any details on any of those."

"So I guess we have the three events, and possibly many more, that seem to indicate that there are occasions when the person possessing the cross encounters a type of power or energy that is hard to understand, but each time this has occurred the cross itself seems to have generated heat ..... or at least it felt warm to the person wearing it," said Raymond. "All of this is certainly beyond my understanding, but since it all seems to relate to the anchor cross, one would have to think, at least, that in each instance a supernatural force intervened. And since I am a follower of Christ I would certainly think that these were occurrences somehow ordained by Him. But truthfully, I guess we just don't know for sure."

Randy nodded, stood, and placed his hand on Raymond's shoulder. "I think that about sums it up, at least for now. Maybe something we find today will shed a little more light on things. You think maybe we should be leaving?"

"Yeah, we don't want to keep Carolyn and Kylie waiting. I know they are as anxious as we are to learn all we can. Let's head out for Mawie's."

Randy and Raymond left the church and drove to Carolyn's mother's home in Wallins. When they arrived there they saw the two ladies sitting in rocking chairs on the front porch, and Kylie was playing in the front yard. Raymond parked his car in the driveway, and the two got out of the car.

"Greetings ladies, and a big greeting to you as well Kylie," said Pastor Bell. "I want you to meet my good friend Dr. Randy Peters who heads up the Center for Appalachia Research at UK in Lexington."

Kylie came running over and gave both men a big hug, and the ladies got out of their chair and shook hands with the men.

Carolyn said, "It is just so good that you've agreed to help us Dr. Peters, and we truly appreciate your driving to Harlan and all your assistance. I feel certain with your knowledge plus that from Pastor Bell we'll gain a lot of understanding today. You ready for a little hike?"

Pastor Bell said, "Let's go!" They all said good-bye to Mawie and the four of them started walking down the path beside the Cumberland River.

After about a half hour they arrived at a point where Kylie said they should leave the river's edge and go into the woods. They all followed Kylie for a while, and then he exclaimed, "There it is! See that old rusty wheel? That's where I found the cross."

Randy said, "Folks, if you agree with me, I suggest that you all stay put where you are and let me go over and look around a bit. If there are human remains here, we'll need to be careful not to disturb things, and we'll have to call the sheriff. The fact is, if there are human bones here we don't really have any way to identify them, or to know how long they've been here, and the circumstances under which they died. That would be a job for the sheriff and detectives to determine. You agree?"

Carolyn, Kylie, and Raymond all nodded in agreement, and they then took a seat on a log and watched Randy start to look around the area.

Randy rummaged carefully through an area about the size of a basketball court. He used a stick to carefully prod, and tried to not disturb things that he located .... just to establish that they were there. After maybe 30 minutes, he came over and sat down beside the three others.

"There's no way I can be sure," he exclaimed. "But I do believe this to be the remains of the wagon belonging to Karl and Mary Seibert. In addition to knowing that Kylie found the golden anchor cross here, I think beyond a doubt this is the site of the remains of an old wagon. It does appear to have been burned. I located one item that looked very much like an old bible ... it had been burned, but pages remained and it certainly appeared to be scripture. There are several other things that could well be of interest. And I can confirm, Kylie, that you were absolutely correct in saying you thought you found human bones. There are definitely two human skulls here in the remains as well as skeletons. And I did notice that there was what appears to be a tomahawk lying atop the rib cage of one of the skeletons. So based on what I've seen, it would be my opinion that this is the remains of the wagon belonging to Karl and Mary Seibert, and that they were likely attacked by Indians, and that the Indians set fire to the wagon when they left."

"That is really something," said Carolyn. "So it would appear that what we have here is not only the place where two people were killed, but also a very significant historical find as well."

"So it would appear," said Randy. "But like I said at the start, since we do have human remains I think the next step would be to relate this story to the local sheriff and let him take it from here."

Kylie's head drooped down, and this was noticed by Pastor Bell, who said, "Kylie, I think I know what you're thinking. I bet you are worried about having to give up the cross."

Kylie just nodded.

Pastor Bell said, "You know, Randy, that I did promise Carolyn and Kylie that I would do all I could to keep anything we found out of the media, and I still think we should try to do that. Our local sheriff is a fine gentleman named J. Bert Sterling. I know that Carolyn has known sheriff Sterling for a long time, and she along with most folks in Harlan County think very highly of him. I would suggest a meeting with Bert to tell him the story about this site. Unfortunately, since the cross was found here I think we should tell him about it. I think that he will agree with us that it should remain with Kylie and that it's his property since he found it, but the sheriff may need to inspect it, take photographs, and even have a lab examine it to establish all they can about it. The down side to this is that the word could leak out that such a beautiful gold cross exists. I think we can certainly make sure no one knows it belongs to Kylie. Do you agree, Randy?"

"I do," Randy replied. "If this does prove to be the remains of the Seiberts and their wagon, then the historical significance is tremendous, and there will be lots of interest and publicity. But other than telling Sheriff Sterling our story, I think we can request, and I think Sheriff Sterling will agree, to not release Carolyn and Kylies names with the story."

Carolyn said, "But if Kylie gets to keep the cross, won't the media want photos of it"

"I'm sure they will," said Randy. "But the sheriff's

office can take these and then release them if they wish .... Kylie would still retain it and no unauthorized person would know he had it."

"Kylie, what do you think?" said Pastor Bell.

"I just know that I really like it," said Kylie. "And I hope I can keep it. I know it is very pretty ..... and valuable, but I like it because it just seems so special to me. I really can't explain my feelings, I just know it's special and I feel special wearing it."

He pulled the beautiful cross from under his t-shirt and held it out in his hand. It was the first time that Randy had seen it. His jaw dropped as his mouth opened. His eyes got large, and he appeared speechless. He reached his hand over next to the cross, and then said, "Kylie, it is magnificent! Could I examine it?"

"Sure thing," said Kylie, and he removed the neck strap and held the cross to Randy.

Randy carefully felt completely over the anchor cross, read the inscription, pax tecum, on it's horizontal arm, and said, "Kylie, I understand completely why you feel so close to this beautiful cross. I'll certainly do all I can to make sure you get to keep it." Randy then returned the cross to Kylie.

"So I guess the next move will be to contact sheriff Sterling," said Raymond. "If you all agree, I'll be glad to meet with him and tell him our story."

"And the sooner the better," said Randy. "We sure don't want anyone to happen onto this site and disturb it before the sheriff gets here. With all our tromping around up here anyone who carefully looked could probably pick up the trail."

All agreed, and with that they started back down to the path beside the river and the walk back to Mawies.

Randy drove Raymond back to his church, and they sat in his car in the church parking lot.

Randy said, "Raymond, it has been some kind of day! Certainly the most exciting I've had in a long time. This whole thing fits so well into my professional life as Director of the Center for Appalachian Research. I would obviously love to be able to document our findings, but in order to do that it would mean they would be available to the public, since UK is a state funded University and nothing produced by its employees can be kept free from public access. So that is a bit of a problem for me. What are your thoughts about it?"

Raymond responded, "It seems to me that the whole thing will become public anyway when the sheriff does his investigation and report. I do believe that Bert will keep Carolyn and Kylie out of his report, and hopefully also the anchor cross. So I would see no problem at all for you to document the historical find at your center. Certainly Carolyn and Kylie would not need to be included in your report, and although the cross might well come up as a question in the future if someone researches Samuel Howard's diary and finds his entries about his friend Karl Seibert, but maybe you could hold off on it until at least things get settled a bit."

"That sounds good," said Randy. "I'll do exactly as you said. My main interest is certainly just in the historical significance of discovering what happened to the Seiberts. Although the stories about the golden anchor cross are beyond interesting, I can certainly hold off on putting any of that in writing for while."

With that Raymond opened the car door and said to Randy before scooting out, "I just don't know how to express my thanks to you for all you've done, but I'll get back with you just as soon as I meet with Sheriff Sterling, and then after all this blows over we'll have to get together somewhere to just get caught up."

"You bet we will, Raymond". And with that Raymond got out, closed the car door and started walking back to his office as Randy began his trip back to Lexington.

18.

Pretty Boy had just arrived in the parking lot at Maggard's grocery. He got out of his car and started into the store.

"Good morning Pretty Boy," said Fatso, as he reached to press the button to open the door going into the back room. "Know what you call an elephant at the North Pole?"

Pretty Boy grunted as he reached to open the back room door.

"You call an elephant at the North Pole lost," yelled Fatso as Pretty Boy entered the back room and closed the door. He then went to his desk, sat down, and put a chew of tobacco in his mouth.

Just a few minutes later Trigger arrived, and as he passed through the grocery store Fatso said, "Hey Trigger, how's it going?" Fatso pressed the button to open the back door for Trigger.

"Not bad so far, Fatso, if I don't have to hear any of your stupid jokes"

To which Fatso replied, "You know what Tarzan said when he saw a herd of elephants?"

Trigger ignored him and entered the back room. "Tarzan said, look, a herd of elephants!" said Fatso with a big giggle.

Trigger grabbed a chair in front of Pretty Boy's desk and said, "I think we could have a problem."

"How's that," said Pretty Boy as he grabbed his cup and spit a stream of brown tobacco juice into it.

"I went to a party last night and got to talking to Julie Lacey from the bank. We all had indulged in a few drinks, so she was speaking pretty freely. She told me Sheriff Sterling had come by Miner's Bank and met with Calvin Brown, and after their meeting the two of them went into the vault. She said she could see them from where she was standing at a cashier's window, and soon as they got into the vault old Calvin started pointing toward our two lock boxes and jabbering away. She said she couldn't hear what they were saying, but she was sure it had something to do with our lock boxes," said Trigger

"They didn't open them, did they?" ask a much more excited Pretty Boy.

"No, no ..... they couldn't do that according to Julie. She said it took a court order to open up a lock box, and even Bert couldn't get one of those without good probable cause. And he sure didn't have that," replied Trigger. "My guess is the money's safe for now, but ole Bert's up to something.

Pretty Boy leaned back in his chair and said, "Yeah, he had to have some reason to be asking questions. I don't think we've screwed up anywhere ..... at least not to my knowledge, but he must have some suspicions. We got about another 10 days or so before we move the money again, and we'll likely need to make several more deposits before then. I think we just need to be extra careful. When you make drop offs to Julie be real sure you don't see the sheriff or any of his deputies hanging around when you park and leave your car. And you probably should try to locate yourself somewhere so you can watch when Julie gets the purse out of your car. I think we're safe ..... no one would suspect her, or be following her, but it wouldn't hurt to be extra careful."

"I can do that, boss," said Trigger. "You think our normal routine for getting the money out of the bank will still be o.k.?"

"Right now I do," said Pretty Boy. "But that thinking could change over the next 10 days."

19.

Ape sat at a table at Creech Cafe drinking a cup of coffee. It was his midafternoon coffee break. He had a package of potato chips open on his table.

"Polly want a cracker, Polly want a cracker," said Polly, perched on the back of a chair beside Ape, who reached into the bag of potato chips and held one out to Polly.

Polly grabbed the chip with her beak and said, "Polly thanks, Polly thanks".

"You're welcome Big Bird," said Ape as he stuffed a handful of chips into his mouth.

Fred Knapp walked by Ape's table and said, "If that bird keeps mooching food she's going to get big as a buzzard." Then he turned to Polly and said, "Quit bothering my customers.....shoo back to your perch." And Fred extended his hand as though he was going to push Polly off the chair. With that Polly flew from the chair back to her perch beside the door and said, "Polly go, Polly go".

Ape said, "Hey Fred, let the bird be, she enjoys both the food and talking to your customers, and I haven't heard any complaints."

Fred nodded, smiled at Ape, and said, "Yeah, Polly's really a pretty good ole bird. I guess we all tolerate her o.k."

The front door opened and in walked Sheriff Sterling.

"Hey Bert," said Fred. "Ape's over at that table," as he pointed toward Ape. "Can I get you a cup of coffee?"

"That would be good, Fred," said the sheriff. "I figured I could find Ape here, and I was needing a break myself," as he strolled over to Ape's table and sat down.

"Anything new?" asked Ape.

"Nothing special," said Bert, as Fred sat a mug of steaming hot coffee in front of him.

Just then about half a dozen youngsters got up from their tables and walked to the cash register to pay Fred for their snacks. School had been out for about an hour, and Creech Cafe was one of their favorite hangouts.

After taking their money, Fred thanked them and then walked over to talk with Bert and Ape.

"I really like these kids, and appreciate greatly their business, but I can't help thinking about how different things are today than when I was their age," Fred said. "Back then we had lots of drive-in restaurants here in Harlan, and most of the kids would find a way to get to one of them to hangout after school and in the evenings. Some had cars and would drive there, others didn't and would hitch a ride with one of their driving friends .... not like that anymore."

Fred thought for a minute, and then pointed to several large framed articles hanging on his wall not far away. "Don't know if you boys ever read that article that I got framed on the wall over there," as he pointed, "but that pretty much sums up how things were in the 1950s with drive-in restaurants and drive-in movies here in Harlan. Some guy wrote that article for the Harlan Daily Enterprise's Heritage Edition recently."

Both Ape and Bert grabbed their coffee cups and walked over beside the article and started to read:

Remembering......Harlan Drive-Ins of the 1950s

In the 1950s there were two kinds of "Drive-Ins" in

Harlan. One was the drive-in theater, and in Harlan there were two of these, the Harlan Drive in and the Wayne Drive In. The other type of drive in was the drive in restaurant (or some called them "custard stands"). There were five of these, Denny Rays, Jacks, Jays, The Dixie, and Mikes. At that time, entertainment for young people centered around these seven Drive-ins. The following are some of my recollections of these Harlan Drive-Ins of the 1950s.

The Harlan Drive-In Theatre was located South of downtown Harlan on highway 421 just prior to getting to the Harlan Regional Hospital, in the Sunny Acres area. I can recall many balmy, summer nights going with friends to the Harlan Drive-In. Often times we would get out of the car, and sit beside it to watch the movie. Most of the time we took food with us, not having enough money to purchase popcorn and sodas at the concession stand. On other occasions, if we were fortunate enough to go to the drive-In with a date, we would opt to stay in the car, and sometimes even watch the movie! Getting passes to the drive-in was always a real treat, and these could sometimes be found. I can recall that when you first got to the drive-in and had entered after dark if you forgot to turn your headlights off upon entering the parking area you could become instantly unpopular by "blinding" those already there and enjoying the movie. When his happened, those thus offended would often start blowing their horns, and quite a scene could be created! In order *to get sound from the movie you needed to park close by a post that had removable speakers that could be attached to your car window. I recall many times wondering through the parking area trying to find a speaker that worked! Others, already parked with a speaker attached, always seemed to find it amusing to watch a car pull up to a speaker that didn't work, try it, and then throw it out the window and move on to try another one! And then as the movie was about to conclude, in order to avoid the big traffic jam one would often leave a bit early. But to do this it was necessary to navigate through the parking area with your lights off, and this could sometimes be a real challenge to avoid hitting something. But all in all, I have very fond memories of going to the Harlan Drive-In.*

The Wayne Drive-In was located off highway 119 a few miles South from Loyall. My most vivid memory of going to the Wayne Drive-In was one summer evening when one of my best friends (I'll leave him un-named, but suffice it to say he is now a very distinguished U.S. federal judge!) and I decided to go, and although we had passes to the theatre we decided it would be more exciting if my friend got in the trunk of my car and slipped into the theatre without paying (and keep in mind that we had passes.....we really wouldn't have had to pay!) We got to the Wayne before dark, I presented my pass and drove on in and found a parking place. After getting all parked, I got out and walked to the back of my car and opened the trunk to let my friend out (in those days cars didn't have trunk releases inside like nowdays). He emerged from the trunk in broad daylight, and we got inside my car. A couple of minutes later there was a rapping on my car window. It was the Wayne theatre's manager coming to ask if I had just let someone out of the trunk of my car. I said yes, but that he had a pass! The manager took a dim view of this and kindly asked us to leave! Pranks such as this one were pretty common at the Harlan Drive-In theaters.

Visits to the drive-in theaters were seldom more than once a week, and more often only once every month or so. On the other hand, visits to the drive-in restaurants were almost nightly...it was the thing to do. And the drive-in restaurants were of two types. One type had both indoor and outdoor service, while the other type only had outdoor, or curb, service.

Denny Ray's Drive-In was located South of Harlan, very close to the Harlan Drive-In theater. It was at the corner off highway 421 at the street that went to the Harlan Appalachian Regional Hospital and the Harlan Smokies Baseball field (now Harlan County High School). Denny Ray's had both inside and curb service. I was fortunate enough to have had my own car in High School. It was a black 1949 model Chevrolet that all my friends referred to as the "Black Bomb". On a typical night I would have two or three of my friends with me and we would go to a drive-in restaurant. If we went to Denny Rays *we would usually go inside to play the pin-ball machines. That was very popular! And of course we would smoke while playing them or while watching our buddies play. Most importantly was watching all the other cars that came there to see if we knew the people, i.e. if they were classmates or others from Harlan High School. At that time Hall High School was open and was close to Denny Rays and lots of kids from Hall High would also be there. If you saw someone you knew, it was usual to walk to the car and have lengthy discussions. Most interesting was the way in which cars departed from the drive-ins. When a car was ready to leave, the driver would first start their engine and gun it several times, signifying to all others that they were getting ready to depart. The driver would then put the car in reverse to back out of the drive-in parking area onto the street. When on the street and still usually rolling backward, the driver would put the car in forward gear, reeve up the motor, and let the clutch out. Then he or she would put the accelerator petal to the floor. All this produced a huge screeching sound and huge amounts of smoke as the tires turned on the pavement. In the 1950s this was called "scratching off", and the louder the screeching and the more the smoke produced the better. Those still at the drive-in would watch and listen with delight (and I'm sure all the automobile mechanics and tire dealers in Harlan approved as well!)*

Jack's Drive-In restaurant was also located on highway 421. If you left Denny Rays driving toward Harlan Jack's was just outside the southern Harlan city limits on the right. In those days the Harlan radio station WHLN was very close to Jacks and across the road. My uncle Estil Giles owned Jacks. It was named for his son, Jack Giles, who now lives in Lexington and is a retired attorney. Unlike Denny Rays, Jacks did not have inside service, only curb. Prior to my high school days my uncle gave me a job at Jacks, my first job! I recall that I started the job as a potato peeler. In those days all food was produced fresh, and French fries were actually made starting with the potato, not the frozen things we get today! Jacks had a potato peeling machine. You probably are not familiar with these, they looked a lot like a concrete mixer, only in miniature. You poured unpeeled potatoes in one end (the end that was tilted up), added water, and then when the machine was turned on it rotated just like a concrete mixer. The inside bottom of the mixer had a very abrasive material on it (like sandpaper) and as the potatoes turned in the water they hit the abrasive bottom which would remove the skin. The real trick was to know how long to leave the potatoes in the tank. If you left them too long more than the skin got removed! I remember several times when I would load the peeler, turn it on, and then forget about it. When I finally did remember, I would find that all that was left was potato soup! My uncle took a dim view of this, and his encouragement made me much more diligent ! It was during those potato peeling days that I also learned how to juggle! Loading the potato machine was pretty boring for a young kid, so I started throwing potatoes up in the air and catching them, just for something to do. Soon I tried to throw more than one, and then finally I got to the point where I could juggle three at a time! I can still do that today, and every time I do I think of those days at Jacks peeling potatoes! After several months on potato duty, my uncle promoted me to wait on customers at the curb (note I hesitate to call myself a "curb girl", but that was the job I had!). After taking an order, the food and drink were placed on a tray that attached to the window of the car. The driver of the car had to roll his or her window down, leaving about 6 inches for the tray attachment. On the bottom of the tray was a pivoted arm that rotated and rested on the outside car door to make the tray level. One of my first orders as a "curb boy" was for a couple of cheeseburgers and chocolate milk shakes. I took the order to the car, asked the driver to roll down the window, and then as I was trying to attach the tray to the window I accidently hit the window with the bottom of the tray, spilling two cheeseburgers and two milk shakes into the drivers lap! I definitely recall that he didn't leave me a tip!! At the back of Jack's was a steep bank that had eroded, and had no vegetation growing on it. My uncle thought this bare bank was unsightly, and asked his son, Jack, and myself to please go to the mountains and gather some nice vegetation to plant on the bank. We took an old pick-up truck and headed for the mountains. We gathered *a whole pick-up truck full of what we thought was a nice looking ivy and took it to the drive-in and planted it on the bare bank. What we had gathered and planted was, in fact, poison ivy! I recall having to be taken to the hospital, and spending about two weeks scratching and healing. Immediately next door to Jacks was a Texaco service station. It was also owned by my uncle Estil Giles, but managed by a nice fellow named Jack Wilson. While Jacks Drive-In did not have inside service, I spent a great deal of time in Jack's Texaco Service Station with Jack Wilson playing pin-ball machines. Most of the money I earned at the drive-in went into the pin-ball machines, 5 cents at a time! One last story about Jack's involved a mechanic that worked at the service station. The mechanic was a very large fellow, and I had gotten to know him well. His name was Bill. One day I walked into the service station and there sat Bill with three hot dogs, a large order of French fries, and a can of Metrocal (for those of you not old enough to remember metrocal it was a milkshake-like canned diet drink). I asked Bill what he was doing. He said, "I'm getting too fat....got to start using this Metrocal to loose weight!". It didn't work!*

Jay's Drive-In restaurant was located in Baxter, just about a mile South of the southern Harlan city limits, just across from the "Coal monument" and just prior to crossing the old bridge (now removed). It was owned by Jay Downs. As I recall, Jays had both inside and curb service. It too was a popular hang-out for kids in the 1950s.

The drive-in restaurants mostly served hamburgers and cheeseburgers, hot dogs, French fries, soft drinks, milk shakes, and cones of "frozen custard" (today very similar to the cones you get at Dairy Queen). They also usually had other sandwiches, such as barbeque, fish, etc., but the burgers, fries, and drinks made up the bulk of their business. Hamburgers were 25 cents, and included all the trimmings. Cheeseburgers were 30 cents, hot dogs with chili were 20 cents, French fries were 15 cents, and milk shakes were 25 cents (and the milk shakes were huge and delicious!).

Further south about a mile on highway 119 from Jays Drive-In was the Dixie Drive-In. It was located in the little community called Lawnville. And then about another mile South was Mike's Drive-In in Loyall. Both the Dixie and Mikes were owned by my uncle Estil Giles (who also owned Jacks, was the Harlan Fire Chief, and owned a taxi business called "900 Cab"). My mother, Lillie Mae (Giles) Edwards managed the Dixie Drive-In, and my father, J.B. Edwards, managed Mike's Drive-In. So the Dixie and Mikes were only about one mile apart, and operated by wife and husband, respectively! I recall there was always lots of competition between the two restaurants. My mother was a very good manager; always hired friendly and efficient personnel, and watched the books very closely. My dad was also an excellent manager, but didn't watch the books as closely as my mother. Dad was loved by all who worked for him and customers alike. His specialty was called a "Mikes Special", and consisted of a loaded cheeseburger, French fries, and onion rings. He probably sold a million of these. I still run into folks today that remind me that they always really liked those "Mikes Specials". Mikes had both inside and curb service, while the Dixie had only curb service. Cody Long was the police chief in the little town of Loyall, where Mikes was located. Cody Long had acquired quite a reputation upholding law and order in Loyall. He spent a lot of time in Mikes Drive-In. He and my dad were very good friends. Because my dad carried fairly large amounts of money each night after he closed Mikes, he carried a small gun. One day while he was in the restaurant the gun fell from his pocket and went off, blowing a hole in the ceiling! Cody Long and many other customers called dad "Barney Fife" (from the old Andy Griffin Show) for a long time after the incident! In order to make some extra money when I was in High School, my mother gave me a job at the Dixie Drive-In to sweep up the trash in the parking lot every morning. You need to understand that in those days everyone threw trash from their cars. This was prior to the litter-bug campaigns ("If you throw litter from your car, you're a litter bug!) If you were driving down the road and eating something that was in paper, or had a paper cup, when finished you just rolled down your car window and threw it out. It was the thing to do. Everyone did it, and no one thought badly about it. At the drive-in restaurants, when finished eating and drinking, you just threw the paper and cups out the window. So after a day and night of business, the parking lot at a drive-in restaurant was absolutely full of trash paper, cups, and uneaten food. My job at the Dixie was to sweep the parking lot prior to the restaurant's daily opening. So this meant I had to get up very early each day. Sweeping the trash each day produced a mountain of paper......and in those days recycling was unheard of!   That's certainly one change today that is for the better! One last story about my dad and Mike's. I went with a friend a few years ago to the Coal Mining Museum in Benham. The lady working there inquired where we were from, and I said Lexington, but that I grew up in Harlan, and then I added that my dad ran Mike's Drive-in in Loyall. To that the lady's eyes got huge, and she said, "Your dad was J.B. Edwards?" I said yes. She then said, "I used to work for J.B., and he was one of the finest men I've ever known. If you ever build a monument for him, contact me and I'll contribute!". That was one of the nicest things anyone has ever said to me.

The five Drive-In restaurants around Harlan are all now gone. One last comment about these restaurants, or custard stands as some would call them. For a town the size of Harlan to have had five drive-in restaurants was truly amazing. I recall one comment about the number of these drive-ins was that someone had decided to build one more, and was going to name it "Custard's Last Stand"! But that didn't happen. All the drive-ins are gone, but the wonderful memories remain!

"Those are good memories," said Bert. "And you are certainly correct, times do change. No more of those drive ins around here today."

Fred and Ape nodded in agreement just as Bert's cell phone rang. He answered it, listened, and then said, "We'll be right over Rosie."

Ape said, "What's Rosie up to Bert?"

"Something's come up, and we need to get back to the office," Bert said as he started for the door with Ape right behind him. They paid Fred and rushed out the door headed for their office across the street.

Bert swung open the door entering the sheriff's office with Ape trailing closely behind. Bert heard the familiar purr, and reached up to stroke Preacher Puss laying on his shelf beside the window and front door. Bert said, "Rosie, what's happening?"

Rosie responded, "Got a call from Pastor Bell saying he was on his way over here to meet with you. Just said it was important, but didn't tell me more than that."

"How long ago was that?" said Bert.

"Been about 15 minutes, he should be here any moment I'd think," responded Rosie

Bert started toward his office and said, "Send him in when he gets here"

"Will do," said Rosie

Just as Bert got into his office and seated his office door opened and in walked Pastor Raymond Bell.

"Bert I appreciate very much your willing to meet with me on such short notice," said Pastor Bell. "I think what I've got for you is very important, and I wanted to waste no time in sharing the information with you."

"Well my friend, lay it on me," said the sheriff.

"It started a few days ago when I received a phone call from Carolyn Potter saying that she and her son Kylie needed to meet with me," said the pastor.

"Oh boy," said the sheriff, "I bet it has to do with that rotten husband of hers."

"I can understand your thinking that," said Raymond. "But actually it does not."

The sheriff looked a bit surprised, and nodded his head.

Pastor Bell continued, "When she got to my office she related to me a story that happened to Kylie. The story is remarkable."

The pastor continued to tell the sheriff the story told him by Carolyn and Kylie about finding the bones and remains from a wagon. At this point he did not mention the golden anchor cross. He then related how he contacted his friend Dr. Randy Peters at UK's Center for Appalachian Research, and shared the information he had received from Randy. He then went on to tell what had happened when Randy visited with them and their visit to the site.

"So if I understand correctly, it is Dr. Peter's conclusion that the remains are those of Pastor Karl Seibert and his wife?" said the sheriff.

"That's right," said Pastor Bell.

"I have a little problem with that," Bert said. "I know there were lots of early settlers that traveled to the area now known as Harlan County. And I'd be willing to bet that quite a few of them didn't make it for one reason or another. I'm sure Indian attacks were frequent, and other accidents and disease caused losses as well. So what specifically makes Dr. Peters think that the remains are those of the Seiberts?"

Pastor Bell looked a little sheepish, and dropped his head a bit and said, "There was one more thing that was found in the remains that I hadn't told you about yet."

"And what was that?" said the sheriff.

"There was a beautiful golden anchor cross that Kylie discovered when he found a hidden compartment bolted onto the bottom of a board that was likely the wagon's seat. The cross appears to be pure gold. It is about 6 inches tall, 4 inches wide, and about a half inch thick. If it is indeed near pure gold it would be worth around $100,000 if someone just melted it down and sold it for today's value of gold. Kylie allowed me to examine and weigh it. It weighs almost 5 pounds! It is truly the most remarkable artifact that I've ever seen, or even read about," said Raymond.

"But I still don't understand what that cross has to do with identifying the remains as those of the Seiberts," said the sheriff.

Raymond continued, "Well, that's where Dr. Peters comes in again. When he heard about the cross it rang a bell for him. His doctorial dissertation was on the history of Harlan County. And he recalled entries in the diary of Samuel Howard that discussed a beautiful golden cross that his friend Karl Seibert possessed. And then in the diary it is recorded that the Seiberts left Williamsburg headed for Mount Pleasant, but never arrived. And Samuel Howard never found out what happened to them."

The sheriff thought a moment and then said, "I can see that that would make the remains more likely to be those of the Seiberts, but there are lots of crosses around. Anything more to identify the cross as belonging to Karl Seibert?"

"Yes, there is," said Raymond. "In Howard's diary he describes the cross as he remembered seeing it when he was with Karl Seibert in Williamsburg before coming to Mount Pleasant. In addition to describing the dimensions and general appearance of the cross, he said it had inscribed on its horizontal member the Latin words pax tecum."

"And I'll bet the cross Kylie found also has these same words on it," said the sheriff.

"It does indeed, Bert", said Raymond.

Raymond again thought for a moment, and said, "I would have to agree that it is highly probable that the remains are those of the Seiberts. But we will still need to have a forensic team from the State Police go to the site and do a bunch of tests on both the bones and the charred materials to try and discover more about them. I could not conclude until getting their report whose remains are there. But I do feel almost sure that your information will help confirm that what Kylie discovered is in fact the remains of the Seiberts and their wagon."

"Which brings us to another sticky point, Sheriff," said Raymond.

"What's that?" said Bert.

"I'm sure you know the big stir this is going to cause when the word gets out," said Raymond. "The press will be all over it, and the media as well as lots of curiosity seekers will descend on Harlan County."

"I suspect you are right, Raymond".

"I'm worried about Carolyn and Kylie. I think we should keep their names out of this for their own protection," said the pastor. "Also, I think the very valuable golden cross should remain with Kylie, and hopefully it would not have to be reported in the story."

"On principle I agree with you," Bert said. "And I do think Kylie will wind up being able to keep the cross. I can't imagine any circumstances that would allow anyone else to claim it. But the existence of the cross will likely have to be a part of my report, and therefore will be public knowledge. They just would not know who had it. Do you think that would work?".

"That's about what I thought you might say," said Raymond. "We'll just have to try and make it work."

The Sheriff stood up and came from behind his desk and shook hands with Pastor Bell and thanked him for bringing forth this information. Bert told Raymond that someone from his office would be visiting him to get all the details, and that he would contact the State Police to get a team of forensic experts to examine the site, and that he would be back with the pastor to set up a visit there when all plans were complete.

Raymond walked to the front door of the sheriff's office and then reached up and gave a good pet to Preacher Puss on his way out.

20.

It was Wednesday, the 19th of June. Bad Eye was sitting at his desk at the junk yard chewing on a cigar. He had just hung up the phone, and he placed a piece of paper on his desk. Snake walked in from outside.

"Bad Eye when are we going to shut this operation down and hear your plans for our retirement?" Snake said.

"Funny you should ask," Bad Eye replied. "I just got off the phone with the Harlan Daily Enterprise giving them information to run in Friday's paper."

"What information," asked Snake.

Bad Eye picked up the piece of paper on his desk and handed it to Snake. It read:

Cawood Junk Yard will close on Saturday, June 22. The owner, Bad Eye Cawood, announced today that the junk yard that has been in his family for two generations will be closing permanently due to declining business. Mr. Cawood said he sincerely regrets having to close the business, but that he had no other alternative. He indicated that all his inventory will be sold for scrap and that he will be listing the property for sale with King Coal Realty. He also stated that he and his three employees were all going to Knoxville to seek employment.

"Wow," said Snake. "That just gives us three days to get everything in order."

Bad Eye sucked on his cigar and grinned at Snake. "We all agreed that we wanted to start our retirement soon as possible," said Bad Eye. "So we've got to get moving. We need to get in all the supplies needed for us to hole up here for about a week, and we need to get all our personal gear that we'll need when we leave the country, including the plane tickets. Once all that is done, then we'll spend the week going over the plans for removing our retirement money from Miner's Bank."

"Sounds like the plan is to hit the bank on Friday, June 28th," Snake said.

"Indeed it is," said Bad Eye. "That's the last day of this quarter, and I figure Pretty Boy will be finished with all his deposits and will be planning to take all his money out sometime after Monday, the first of the month. In addition, the bank will likely be holding an extra amount of cash in order to meet first of the quarter demand. It seems like the right time for us to make our move."

Bad Eye continued, "So you tell Jones and Billie what I've just told you, and you three start to get all the supplies in here that we'll need for the week. If all goes as planned I'll hang up a CLOSED sign on our gate this Saturday. Then we'll just lay low and go over in detail our plans for Friday the 28th."

"I'm on it Boss," said Snake as started out to look for Jones and Billie.

21

Fatso was watching a soap opera on tv. Trigger walked in the grocery store and started across to the door to the back room.

"Plush the button Fatso," Trigger shouted.

As he pushed the button to allow Trigger into the back room Fatso replied, "Morning Trigger Man, know what's grey and puts out forest fires?"

Trigger groaned.

"Smoky the Elephant," giggled Fatso as Trigger slammed the door.

Pretty Boy was pouring himself a cup of coffee as Trigger entered the room.

"Want a cup of mud," said Pretty Boy.

"Yeah, that sounds good," replied Trigger as he grabbed a mug and started to pour his coffee. Pretty Boy returned to his desk. The two sat facing each other.

Pretty Boy said, "I been doing more thinking about the sheriff nosing around at the bank looking at our lock boxes. I still can't understand how he could have any idea of our operation, but I know something's up. We only got a little over a week before the end of the quarter, so just to be on the safe side I've contacted all our dealers and told them to not bring us more money until next quarter. I think they can all hold their money that long without any trouble. We've already stashed over 3 million dollars in those two boxes since our last trip to Knoxville. We don't want to take any chances of losing that. So if the sheriff somehow comes up with some way to open our lock boxes after Monday, July 1 he'll just find empty boxes. We'll clean em out and take the money to Knoxville on Monday morning, July 1. Then we'll just have to be extra careful with our deposits after that."

"Short of changing our operation around completely somehow, that sounds like a good plan Pretty Boy," said Trigger as he sipped his coffee.

Pretty Boy finished his coffee and then grabbed a pinch of tobacco and put it in his mouth. He nodded slowly, and after a bit spit a stream of tobacco juice into his Styrofoam cup.

Trigger got up and walked back to the computer and

checked his email. Pretty Boy continued to think about sheriff Sterling's interest in his lock boxes at the bank.

22.

Sheriff Sterling and Deputy Cornett were walking across the street from their offices to Creech Cafe. As they entered the cafe they heard the familiar voice, "Polly want a cracker, Polly want a cracker." The sheriff looked up at the bird and said, "Polly can just keep on wanting.... we're just here for coffee and I know you don't drink the stuff."

"Polly sad, Polly sad, Polly sad," said the bird.

Bert and Ape chose a table and sat. Bert said, "We can't stay long Ape, we have a meeting coming up at 10:30 this morning with Pastor Bell and the state police forensic unit to let them take a look at the site where Kylie found the remains. I'm still concerned about trying to keep Carolyn and Kylie out of public knowledge, and I think it important that we do all we can to accomplish that."

"I agree sheriff," said Ape. "Not only would it cause them all kinds of trouble from the press and curiosity seekers, but if word got out that they had that golden cross they might get visits from robbers out to steal it for just it's value when melted down and sold. And that would really be tragic. Not only could Carolyn or Kylie get hurt, but the true value of the cross as an artifact from hundreds, if not thousands, of years ago would be lost."

Bert nodded, "True, so it's up to us to protect them, and to keep the cross and the two of them safe from harm. We just have to remember to be very careful not to let their names slip out when meeting with the media or talking with the public."

Fred Knapp strolled over to Bert and Ape's table and said, "We got some good fresh doughnuts, boys."

"Not for me Fred, just coffee," said the sheriff.

"Ditto," said Ape.

Fred left for a few minutes and returned with two steaming hot cups of coffee. As he sat them on the table he noticed Ape looking over the head of Bert at one of his hundreds of framed photos mounted on the store walls.

"Know what that photo's about?" Fred asked Ape.

Ape replied, "Well, it caught my eye because it is a bit unusual. It looks like a man standing just outside the door of a home with one of his feet stomping on a box that looks like it's on fire. And there's a lot of mucky

looking brown goo squirting out of the box! Beats me....
but I know you're going to explain it Fred."

Fred started, "It happened maybe 20 years ago. It
was all just a prank that a couple of kids wanted to play on
one of their teachers at Harlan High School. One of the
kids lived in the county, and his family had horses. So they
got this shoe box and filled it with horse manure. Then
they waited until it was dark and slipped to the door of
their biology teacher, Mr. Perry. They then poured a little
charcoal starter fluid on the box and set it on fire, rang
the doorbell, and ran and hid behind a tree in the front
yard. Perry comes to the door, opens it, and is terrified
to see some kind of box on fire on his porch. He wanted
to quickly put out the fire, so he started stomping on the
box. When he did the manure flew out of the box all
over his pants and shoes. That's the brown stuff you see
in the photo. Now here's the unbelievable part. The kids
brought a camera and wanted to take a picture to show
to their friends at school. They did take the picture, and
I must admit it's a good one. But then when the Harlan
City Police got into the investigation they discovered that
the picture was circulating at the school, and it didn't
take them long to find who it belonged to. Those kids got
some very strict disciplinary measures applied to them.....
I think they got suspended from school for a semester
and also had to apologize to Mr. Perry. The newspaper
managed to get a copy of the picture, and ran it with

an article describing what happened. I just framed the picture and hung it on my wall."

"Hey, that is some story," said Ape. "And I know I shouldn't say this, but it had to really be funny! The kids should have taken a video! Seeing ole Mr. Perry stomping away on that box and watching the shit fly all over him would have been something to behold."

The sheriff said, "Ape, you're right, you shouldn't think of a sick stunt like that as funny." And then the sheriff got a big grin on his face, and all three started laughing so hard that tears rolled down their cheeks.

Bert then glanced at his watch, and said, "Hey Ape, we got to be getting back to the office to meet Pastor Bell and the state investigators."

Bert and Ape paid Fred for the coffee and headed back across the street to the sheriff's office.

As they walked in the door they each reached up and stroked Preacher Puss and were rewarded with a loud meow and big swish of her tail.

"Everyone's already in your office sheriff," said Rosie. "I already got them coffee. I know you just had some, so I guess you're good."

"Thanks Rosie," said the sheriff as he and Ape opened the door into his office.

Seated around the sheriff's desk were Pastor Bell and two detectives from the Kentucky State Police's forensic unit. They introduced themselves as Bennie & Charlie. The sheriff and Ape took their seats.

"Appreciate you all coming," Bert said. He then described for the benefit of the detectives the story of Kylie's finding the ruins without mentioning Kylie by name. The sheriff then asked Pastor Bell to pick up how he came to be involved and to describe the input he received from Dr. Peters. Raymond told of these events, and then told about the beautiful golden cross, and how Samuel Howard's diary had pegged the ruins to likely be those of Karl and Mary Seibert.

The detectives slowly nodded and each entered the information into their log books. Bennie then looked up and said, "Well, I guess we need to get out there and take a look around. It sure sounds like all the evidence points to the remains being those of the Seiberts, but we can make it official."

And with that the five of them left the sheriff's office, got in the State Police cruiser, and started toward Wallins.

Sheriff Sterling had decided not to mention or involve Carolyn, Kylie, or Mawie in any way. So he directed Charlie, driving the car, to a remote parking area that was about one mile from the site of the Seibert remains. There was a path that then lead them down close to the Cumberland River, and it joined the path that ran parallel to the river that Kylie had followed previously. Then they got to the spot where they left the path and walked a ways into the woods until they reached the remains.

Pastor Bell carefully pointed out the old wagon wheels, the charred remains of the seat that contained the hidden compartment, and the two sets of human bones. Raymond and Ape then walked over to a log and sat down while the sheriff and the two detectives closely examined the site for the next two hours. Photographs were taken of everything that could be identified of interest. The detectives then gathered all items that seemed associated with the wagon, labeled them, and put them carefully into evidence bags. All of the bones were gathered and each set was placed in a body bag.

"I think we're finished," Bennie said.

Pastor Bell and Ape stood up, stretched, and helped the other three carry all the bags and equipment back to the car. They then drove back to the sheriff's office in Harlan.

After parking at the back of the sheriff's office, all five got out of the car.

Charlie said, "It'll take a few days for us to run tests on all this stuff, and after we've done that we'll get back with you with the results. Looks for sure to me like we have the remains of the Seiberts and their belongings, but we'll have to wait for the reports to be certain."

"Sounds good," Bert responded. "Thanks again for all your help, and we'll look forward to seeing what you come up with."

Charlie & Bennie got back in their car and pulled away leaving the sheriff, Ape, and Pastor Bell standing in the parking lot.

"What's your thoughts Raymond?" asked the sheriff.

"Thought it went good sheriff," replied Pastor Bell. "I was surprised they didn't ask for the golden cross, but I guess our statements about it seemed to satisfy them. Although I wouldn't be too surprised if they wanted to see it before it's all over."

"My thoughts as well," Bert said. "I think they realize that the cross is quite valuable and that someone has it and wants to remain anonymous.....and I think they trust our judgment about it. And it wouldn't add anything new to their investigation, given that they have our detailed statements about the cross. So maybe we will be able to let Kylie keep it, and keep it from the media."

Ape said, "Yeah, I think all went as well as could be expected. I just hope they don't come back with something unreasonable."

"Let's call it a day!" Bert responded. And the three nodded in agreement as they each headed for their cars.

23.

It was Friday, June 21. Julie Lacey had just returned from lunch, and approached Carolyn Potter standing behind a teller's window at the Miners Bank.

Julie said, "Carolyn, I'm so sorry to hear that Snake has lost his job at the Junk Yard. Does he know what he's going to do?"

Carolyn got a surprised look on her face and replied, "Julie, I didn't know he lost his job... how did you know?"

"Oh, I'm so sorry. I thought you knew. I read about it in today's Enterprise. The article just said that business was too bad to continue and that Bad Eye was closing it down as of tomorrow. It also said that all the employees were going to Knoxville to look for jobs," Julie replied.

"Snake is just a difficult man to live with, Julie," said Carolyn. "He doesn't share a lot with me, and, as I'm sure you know, still drinks a lot. It is a rare time that he is sober and wants to talk with me about anything of substance. I'll just have to confront him with this development tonight and see what I can find out. I appreciate very much your sharing the information with me."

"Oh, you're most welcome. I'm just sorry things are not going better for you at home," said Julie as a customer approached her teller window with a deposit in hand. Carolyn was dreading already the conversation she must have with her husband this evening.

School was out for the summer, but Kylie stayed in Wallins with his grandmother Mawie during the day while his mother worked.   The two loved each other dearly, and Kylie enjoyed being at his grandmother's house. He liked to sit and talk with his grandmother, and also liked playing both indoors and out. Today he had gone for a long walk along the path beside the Cumberland River. It was so beautiful. Everything was in bloom, and the trees and grass were such a lovely green. He even noticed some trailing arbutus blooming among the rocks at the river's edge. And the water in the river was so cool and clear, as it passed over rocks and boulders. Kylie remembered reading in his history books about how pristine everything was at the time the pioneers settled in Harlan County, and then during the years that followed many became careless with their trash, and the Cumberland River became polluted with all kinds of stuff

..... from cars and refrigerators to thousands of different kinds of plastics, cans, and papers. Then in the later part of the 20th century folks became more conscious of their environment. The river was cleaned up, and people did not pollute as they had before. The Cumberland River was now back to almost pristine conditions in most places. And Kylie certainly did enjoy walking along the river bank and enjoying all it's natural beauty. He would occasionally pick up a rock and toss it into the river. Sometimes he would find one that was flat and he would try and make it skip across the surface of the water. Other times he would wind-up and make his longest toss to try and get a rock to sail across the river.... but mostly those rocks fell short of the land on the other side. Kylie was always on the lookout for fish in the river, and sometimes he spotted them.

The river was really special to Kylie. As he was walking today back to Mawie's house he thought about the time a few years back that he had studied in school how all the rivers ran into other rivers and eventually into the oceans. He got the idea that if he threw a bottle with a note in it into the river that it would eventually flow all the way to the ocean, then around the world, and then one day it would come back down the Cumberland River and he might see it and get it back. He even thought that someone in some foreign land might get his note in the bottle and write something to him in return. So

Kylie wrote a note, put it in a bottle, placed the lid on the bottle, and threw it into the Cumberland River and watched as it floated away. He didn't know how long it might take for his bottle to make it all around the world and back, but he thought it would be at least a month. So a month after tossing it into the river, Kylie went down and walked along the riverbank every day looking for his bottle. When he didn't find it, he told his story to Mawie one day. His grandmother told him that the bottle might indeed make it all the way to the ocean, and maybe even around the world, but that it couldn't get back into the Cumberland River. After Mawie's explanation Kylie thought about it and then understood. So he finally stopped looking for his bottle, but still enjoyed greatly looking at the beautiful Cumberland River.

Kylie got back to Mawie's house just as his mother drove up in the driveway.

"Hi mom," shouted Kylie.

"Hi sugar," Carolyn said. "Run in the house and tell Mawie I'm here and picking you up, and then hurry back."

Kylie did so, and then as they pulled out of the driveway Mawie walked out on the front porch and waved goodbye to them. Carolyn honked the horn and they both waved back.

Carolyn and Kylie got home, and Carolyn had just finished fixing dinner when she heard Snake drive up and slam his truck door. She had dreaded this encounter, and she had prayed that he would be sober and would talk with her about his plans now that the junk yard was closing. Kylie was in his room studying before dinner.

Snake walked in the front door and said, "Hope dinner's ready .... I'm hungry as a bear".

Carolyn met him in the living room and said, "Dinner's all ready dear, but could I talk with you a minute before we eat?".

"Make it damn quick," he said.

"I understand from an article that was in today's Enterprise that the junk yard is closing tomorrow and everyone will be losing their jobs," Carolyn said.

"Yeah, been meaning to tell you about that. Just found out yesterday, and last night, as you know, I was a bit under the weather. Bad Eye had to shut it down, and all four of us are going to Knoxville to look for jobs. I'll pack tonight. Don't know how long I'll be gone."

Carolyn was shocked that Snake was actually talking to her, and was secretly pleased that he planned to leave for a while. "We'll miss you honey," she said. "But you be sure to call to check-in every few days or so."

"Do what I can," said Snake. "Let's eat."

Carolyn called for Kylie and the three of them had dinner.

24.

Bert and Ape were sitting at the counter at Creech Cafe drinking coffee. Fred Knapp walked over with a carafe full of hot coffee and filled their cups.

Bert said, "Fred, I'm still giggling over that story about Mr. Perry stomping on that flaming box."

"Yeah," Fred said. "Kids back then did lots of pranks. Most of them weren't really malicious, but they could get pretty nasty. Another one that happened frequently here in Harlan related to the coal "shoots" as they were called. These were the long, round tubes made of metal that conveyed coal. Homes that were located on hills, as most are around here, often had these "shoots" going from a street behind their property down to their home or coal storage house. So when the homeowner needed a load of coal to burn in his furnace for heat, he would place an order and a truck would come on the street behind him and shovel the coal into the "shoot" and let gravity do it's thing as the coal went down the conveyor to the homeowners basement coal bin or to a coal storage house. The prank that kids often did was to find a pretty good size rock, usually a big round one, and after everyone had gone to bed at night go to the top of the "shoot" and heave the big boulder into the shoot. By the time it got to the bottom it had up a pretty good head of steam, and the kids really got their kicks from listening to it crash through the coal storage building or into the coal bin in the basement of the house. Lots of damage was done with that prank."

Fred continued, "And then another one was to fill balloons with water and to drive around and find someone, often times an elderly man or woman, walking down the street and as the kids would drive by they would roll down the passenger side window and toss one of these water filled balloons at the person. Often the person would see what they first thought was just a balloon and stick out their hands to catch it, and then would get plastered all over with water as the balloon burst."

"We catch anyone doing either of those pranks today they would wind up in jail," Ape commented. "They might be meant just for fun, but they could have some serious consequences."

"Oh, Ape, you just got no sense of humor," said the sheriff with a smile on his face.

Fred walked off to pour coffee for other customers.

The sheriff and deputy walked back across the street to their offices. As soon as they walked in the door Rosie said, "Mail's here", and handed the sheriff a bundle of mail.

Bert noticed a large envelope that had Post 10 of the Kentucky State Police as the sender. He figured that was the report from Charlie & Bennie on the wagon remains. He went into his office, got comfortable at his desk, and opened the envelope. Ape sat across from him and watched quietly as the sheriff read the report.

After several minutes the sheriff put the report down, looked at Ape, and said, "About what we expected. They say the tests done on the bones determined that they were at least a couple of hundred years old and that there were marks on the bones that supported the cause of death as being likely from Indian attack. Also, the charred remains of a bible revealed the name Karl Seibert on one of the pages. Everything else lends support to our story of the wagon remains being those from the Seiberts. They did include our story about the golden anchor cross being found attached to the bottom of the charred wagon seat, and also the report given to us from Pastor Bell and his friend Dr. Peters about Samuel Howard's diary discussing the trip to be made by the Seiberts, and the detailed description of Karl Seibert's golden anchor cross that Samuel Howard himself had examined while with Seibert at Williamsburg."

"So they concluded the remains were definitely those of the Seiberts, and we got by without any mention of Carolyn and Kylie?' asked Ape.

"Sure did," said the sheriff. "Course the real test will come when the press gets hold of this. They'll want to see the cross, and want to know who has it. We'll just have to keep a lid on that information."

"How do you plan on releasing the story, Bert?" asked Ape.

"I think we're forced to call a press conference," Bert replied. "I don't like those things, but in this case it's going to be big news and we need to handle it right. Tomorrow's Saturday. How about you ask Rosie to send out a notice to all the usual media that we'll have a press conference tomorrow at 10 am here in the sheriff's office to address the murder of two people as well as a very significant historical finding. I'm sure that will get their interest."

"Bet it will," said Ape.

Then Bert continued, "And I'll call Pastor Bell and see if he and hopefully Dr. Peters can make the press conference tomorrow. I think they could help a lot with the questions that will be asked."

"That's good Bert," Ape replied. "That should cover about all our bases."

25.

Saturday morning was one of those really beautiful, refreshing times. The mountains were in full bloom, the temperature had cooled during the night, the humidity was very low due to a breeze out of the North, the skies were crystal clear, and as the sun began to filter through the trees it's golden rays struck dew drops on their leaves to yield rainbows of color. Mother nature at its best.

Bad Eye was at the gate leading into the junk yard with a large hand lettered sign that said CLOSED. He was taping the sign onto the gate with duct tape (commonly referred to in Eastern Kentucky as Tennessee Chrome). After affixing the sign he closed the gate, and then headed up the gravel road back to the junk yard.

"Get the sign on the gate?" asked Snake.

"All done," responded Bad Eye. "We is now officially closed."

All four had been gathering supplies into the junk yard for the past three days. They had accumulated enough food to last them for a week, and they had each gathered their personal belongings that they thought they would need for their "retirement trip". In addition, they got their passports, and plane tickets out of the country. Bad Eye had elected to fly to Nassau in the Bahamas. He had visited there years ago and had always thought he'd like to spend a lot more time there. Snake had elected to fly into the Bahamian island of Great Abaco. He would fly to Marsh Harbor and then take the Ferry over to the small island of Man-O-War Cay. He had heard all about this place from a friend that had traveled there frequently. It sounded exactly like what he wanted. Jones Anderson had elected to travel to Marsh Harbor with Snake, but then to take the ferry over to Hopetown on Elbow Cay. Snake had told Jones the stories he had heard about the beautiful Abacos and was delighted when Jones planned to go there too. But Snake told him that they had to go to different islands so they would have less chance of being discovered. Billie Lingel had decided on the British Virgin Islands. His parents had traveled there and had told Billie all about how wonderful the islands were. His plan was to fly to Tortola and catch the ferry to the island of Virgin Gorda where he had rented a cottage.

All four were getting very excited about the prospects of a great worry free retirement in paradise. They had decided to ride together to the Knoxville airport, and each had purchased plane tickets leaving from there. They had decided to take Billie's car. It was in better shape than any of those belonging to the other three.

Their plan was to drive to Knoxville and park in one of the downtown parking lots, switch the license tags with those from another car in the parking lot, and then catch a cab to the airport. Each of the four had purchased false passports and identity papers from a fellow junk yard owner in Pineville, Kentucky that had good connections to procure such documents.

So, their plan was coming together. All they had to do now was rob the Harlan Miners Bank of all its money and make a clean get away to Knoxville.

Bad Eye had gathered the other three into the junk yard office. It was about 8 am on Saturday morning.

"Well, well, well," said Bad Eye. "I think we're right on track with our retirement plans. The junk yard is officially closed. We've gotten in supplies for a week's hide out here. And we've gotten everything we need to travel out of the country. Now we need to talk about our plan to extract our retirement cash from Harlan Miners Bank."

"I hope it ain't too complicated Bad Eye," said Billie. "I ain't too smart and if it's hard I might screw up."

"Been thinking about it awhile, Billie," replied Bad Eye. "And the plan I have will work. You just do as you're told and we'll walk out of that bank with about all the money we can carry, and be on easy street for the rest of our lives."

Billie, Jones, and Snake all smiled and nodded agreement.

Bad Eye continued, "Now here's what we're going to do next Friday. The bank closes at 4:30. I want Jones to go in the bank about 5 minutes before it closes. He don't spend a lot of time in town, and no one's going to pay any attention to him. Sometimes there are customers in the bank at closing time, and the bank's president, Calvin Brown, will walk to the door and turn the sign to read CLOSED at exactly 4:30 so that no one else will enter. Jones will be standing at a table pretending to fill out a deposit slip and will take his time.....acting like he's got a lot of checks to deposit. He'll take a lot of old checks I'll give to him to make it look good. He'll watch until the last customer leaves the bank, and then he'll start toward a teller's window with his deposit. The guard on duty will be Gut Blankenship. As you all know, old Gut is in his 70s, can't hear, and is blind as a bat. He's 5 foot 5 inches tall and weighs 300 pounds. As Jones passes close to Gut he'll draw his derringer from under the deposit papers and stick it to the side of Gut's head and shout to the others in the bank that if they make any move he'll shoot Gut then and there. Gut won't resist. He won't be a problem. Then Jones will open the door for the three of us. We'll be standing just outside talking to each other like we had just met. Our car will be parked right beside us, and I'll have a box of trash bags with me. When Jones opens the bank door we'll calmly walk into the bank, shut the door, and lock it. The CLOSED sign will still be showing. We can then start the business of extracting the cash."

"What if we can't get a parking space next to the bank entrance Bad Eye?" asked Snake.

Bad Eye said, "I've watched those parking spaces at 4:30 for the past week. As you know, downtown Harlan has really gone South. Not much going on there anymore. At the time the bank closes there have never been cars parked along the street close to the bank entrance. And even if there was one or two, we could always find one close enough that would work."

"What are the trash bags for Bad Eye?" asked Jones.

Bad Eye responded, "They're for our retirement money, Jones. We will all be dressed like maintenance men, including you. When we walk out of the bank with big trash bags we'll just look like janitors cleaning the bank. If anyone saw us they wouldn't become alarmed."

"Who will be in the bank Bad Eye," asked Billie.

"There should only be three people other than Gut," answered Bad Eye. "Calvin Brown, Julie Lacey, and Carolyn Potter. Julie and Carolyn should be no problem. They'll both be at a tellers window and will do exactly as Jones said. Brown is the one we've got to be careful about. He could be anywhere, but likely he'll have walked back to his office after turning over the CLOSED sign at 4:30. Jones will have a good view of him in his office, and will have to make sure that he doesn't try something smart. The three of us will enter almost as soon as Jones sticks the gun on Gut, and I want Billie to run to Brown's office just as soon as he gets into the bank. He'll put a gun on Brown and keep him under control. Me and Snake will watch Julie and Carolyn. Jones will have a rope in his pocket and tie Gut's hands behind his back and take his gun. Frankly, I doubt it has bullets in it, and even if it does they are probably so old they wouldn't fire anyway. Jones then makes Gut sit on the floor. In his condition he would never be able to stand up with his hands tied behind him, so we don't have to worry any more about him."

Bad Eye continued, "One thing I forgot to mention is that the three of us slip on ski masks just before we enter the bank. I don't think anyone will recognize Jones, since he's seldom in town and spends all his time at the junk yard. But the three of us would be recognized immediately, and that could cause a problem. Especially if Carolyn saw Snake. She might do anything.....so I want to avoid that. A little later on it won't matter if we're identified. I've talked with Snake about this, and he's in agreement. But initially we put on the ski masks. They'll keep us from being recognized when we first come in the bank. I'll then demand that the ladies bend over and put their faces down on the surface in front of them. Then they won't be able to see us. Me and Snake will walk around behind the teller's cages and tie the ladies' hands behind their back. Then we'll put blindfolds on them. We'll carry those and the ropes in our pockets. Then we make the ladies lie on the floor. While we're doing that, Billie will demand Calvin Brown produce the special pass key to the safe deposit boxes. Billie will tell him that unless he does we'll start shooting his three employees, one at a time until he produces the pass key. And then if he still hasn't produced it we tell him his time on Earth has ended and we shoot him."

"If that happens, how we gonna get in the safe deposit boxes?" asked Snake.

"It won't happen," said Bad Eye. "He'll produce it before we have to do any shooting. He don't want to have anyone killed if he can avoid it."

Bad Eye went on, "So then after we get the pass key we tie up Brown and blindfold him. Then we sit him down in his chair and tie him to the chair. We can watch the ladies from the vault. We go in the vault, empty the lock boxes into our trash bags, and then come out and get all the bank cash. Just one thing left to do before we head to the car. We get all four of the employees and put them in the vault and close and lock it."

"They'll never make it alive in there over the weekend Bad Eye," said Billie.

"Can't be helped," said Bad Eye. "They will have recognized our voices or mannerisms or something by then, and we can't take the chance of being identified. As I told you, I talked with Snake about this before, and he was o.k. with it. It's just part of doing business. By the time they are found on Monday morning we'll be sitting in paradise counting our money."

Bad Eye looked at each of the three. They all nodded slowly in agreement, and then a smile formed on each of their faces.

Bad Eye continued, "We'll go over this plan many times before next Friday. We'll make sure everyone knows exactly what to do when. We'll have everything down pat. What do you think?"

Snake said, "Sounds good to me. I kind of hate to have to do in the old lady, but that's just the way it goes." Billie and Jones nodded in agreement.

26.

Dr. Randy Peters and Pastor Raymond Bell arrived at the sheriff's office at 9:30 am on Saturday morning. They were each greeted with a big meow as they walked in the door. Raymond reached up and stroked Preacher Puss, and then said, "Hi Rosie, I would like you to meet my good friend from Lexington, Dr. Randy Peters. Randy's the Director of the Center for Appalachian Research at U.K."

"So pleased to meet you Dr. Peters," said Rosie.

"And I'm most pleased to meet you Rosie. Please call me Randy"

"Bert and Ape are getting all set up in the evidence room for the press conference. They thought there would be more room in there. Please go right in," said Rosie.

Randy and Raymond proceeded into the evidence room which was set up with a podium at one end of the room with about a dozen chairs in front of it. Sheriff Sterling was at the podium checking the microphone, and Ape was finishing up arranging the chairs. The shelves for evidence storage lined both side walls, so the room worked well for the press conference.

"Hey Sheriff and deputy, how you both?" said Pastor Bell.

"Doing great Raymond, and Randy we really are again glad to see you and appreciate so much your driving down from Lexington....you had to get up pretty early this morning," commented the sheriff.

"Not too early," said Randy. "Left Lexington about 6:30 ..... takes me about two and a half hours. I'm just pleased to be included and just hope I can be of assistance."

"I'm sure you will," said Bert. Just then the door swung open and a troop of people started entering the room. Bert told Randy and Raymond to take a seat, and then went to meet the visitors.

"Hi sheriff," said a man dressed in a coat and tie. "I'm Tim Bates, reporter for the Knoxville News-Sentinel. This fellow beside me here is my good friend and competitor Blake Johnson with the Lexington Herald-Leader. We appreciate your inviting us, and look forward to hearing all about this."

"Thanks guys," said the sheriff. "Have a seat and we'll get underway shortly."

Next in was a television crew, complete with camera man and reporter. A smartly dressed lady stuck out her hand to the sheriff and said, "I'm Barbara Clark with WKYT television in Lexington. The fellow with the camera there is Sam Jenkins. If it's o.k. with you we'll go ahead and get all set up."

"Sure thing," the sheriff said.

"Hey Bert, looks like something's cooking," said A.J. Sampson. He was a reporter for the Harlan Daily Enterprise, and well known to Bert.

"Yeah, A.J., I guess you could say that. You doing o.k.?" said the sheriff

"Real fine," said A.J. as he took a seat.

Ape walked over to the sheriff and said, "Bert, looks like this is the audience. I've got a couple of minutes past 10. So I guess you could go ahead and get underway." Ape then took a seat.

Bert walked to the podium and said, "I think I've met each of you. I appreciate your taking the time to be here today. I think what we've got is very important, and I feel it will be of great interest to those you represent. Before we get started, let me introduce three other people. The deputy there in the back of the room is Ape Cornett. The two gentlemen sitting here at the front are Pastor Raymond Bell from the New Hope Baptist Church here in Harlan, and Dr. Randy Peters, Director of the Center for Appalachian Research at the University of Kentucky in Lexington." Raymond and Randy each stood and waved as they were introduced.

Just then the door swung open and two officers of the Kentucky State Police entered the room.

The sheriff said, "And the two gentlemen just entering the room are from the Kentucky State Police. They are Bennie Long and Charlie O'Conner." Bennie and Charlie waved to everyone and took a seat beside Randy and Raymond.

"To start off, I think we need to give you a brief history lesson," Bert said. "You'll understand why this is necessary shortly. We could not have anyone more qualified to talk about the history of Harlan County than Dr. Peters. So Randy, if you could bring us up to speed on what happened way back there at the end of the 18th century that's pertinent to this story today."

Randy stood and took the podium as Bert continued to stand at the side.

"Thanks sheriff," said Randy. "You may already be aware that before it was known as Harlan the founding pioneer Samuel Howard and his family settled here in 1796 and called it Mount Pleasant. Samuel Howard had come here from Williamsburg. While he was at Williamsburg he met a fellow that became a good friend named Reverend Karl Seibert. Seibert had immigrated from Germany. In 1796 Howard and his family traveled to Kentucky and became the first to settle at what he called Mount Pleasant, now called Harlan. After a couple of years he wrote to his friend Reverend Seibert asking him to come to Mount Pleasant to start a church. Seibert agreed, and after marrying his wife Mary, began the journey in 1798."

"How do we know this Dr. Peters?" shouted Blake Johnson with the *Lexington Herald-Leader*.

"Good question," Randy responded. "Samuel Howard kept a very detailed and precise diary, and the information I've just given you, and that which you will hear shortly, are based on entries in that diary. The original diary is presently located at the Center for Appalachian Research at UK."

"Thank you," said Blake Johnson

"The last thing I'll say right now is that the Seiberts never did reach Mount Pleasant. Samuel Howard did get a letter from Karl Seibert saying he and Mary were going to come, but that was the last he heard from him."

The sheriff again stood at the podium and Dr. Peters took a seat. Bert then said, "Well, that's the necessary history lesson. Now we fast forward to about a month ago. A person that will remain anonymous was hiking in the woods a few miles from Wallins. This person happened upon what looked like an old rusty wheel sticking a bit up out of the ground, and started to pry around, and found another wheel and some charred boards. He then started digging around the area and came across some bones that looked human. He left the area, and later contacted his pastor, Raymond Bell for advice. Raymond maybe you can pick it up here."

Pastor Bell and Bert exchanged places, and Pastor Bell said, "After meeting with the gentleman I was very fascinated with his story. I myself have a great interest in the history of this area, being a history major in college. Dr. Peters is a dear friend that I met while teaching in Lexington, and I knew that he was an expert on the history of Harlan County, having written his doctorate dissertation on this subject. So I called him and told him the story the gentleman had related to me. He was so fascinated that he wanted to drive to Harlan and join us when we went to the site to investigate further. So myself, Dr. Peters, the gentleman that found the site, and another anonymous person went to the site for examination. It didn't take long to establish that there were, in fact, human remains there and that there appeared to be old charred remains of what could be a wagon. We did not want to further disturb the site, so at that point I was elected to contact Sheriff Sterling to tell him what we had found and seek his advice. After hearing the story, Sheriff Sterling said we should contact the Kentucky State Police and have them send a team of forensic detectives to accompany us back to the site of the remains. I'll let Sheriff Sterling take it again from here."

Raymond sat and the sheriff again stood at the podium.

"One thing that has not been addressed thus far is that a beautiful golden anchor cross was found initially when the first person on the site was sifting through the charred wood. This cross was found in a locked compartment on the bottom of a piece of charred wood that likely was the wagon seat. In Samuel Howard's diary he described the cross exactly. Karl Seibert had shown it to him while the two of them were in Williamsburg. When Pastor Bell mentioned the cross to Dr. Peters he remembered reading about it in the diary. That was the first indication that the ruins we found were likely from the Seiberts and their wagon. This information was passed on to the State Police, and the next thing that happened was for us all to return to the site in order for the forensic detectives to properly examine everything. So I'll let one of them take over now." Bert again sat down and Bennie Long came to the podium with a report in hand.

Bennie began, "Everything was as told by Sheriff Sterling. We arrived at the site of the ruins and Charlie O'Conner and I made a thorough examination of everything we could find and thought might be pertinent. We physically examined things, took photographs, made measurements, and bagged and labeled everything. The human bones were carefully moved into a body bag. All this evidence was then brought back and tests performed. I have a copy here of our report, and Charlie has several additional copies for each of you. The bottom line is that we have concluded the bones are those belonging to Karl and Mary Seibert. The other remains appear to be what's left of their wagon and personal belongings. In proximity to each of the skeletons was found arrow heads and a tomahawk head. We have thus concluded that the Seiberts were, in all likelihood, killed by a band of roving Indians and their wagon set on fire. About the only item of interest we salvaged other than the golden anchor cross, was a bible that was badly charred, but our lab was able to make out Karl Seibert's name on one page. So, we think we know the ruins to be those of Karl and Mary Seibert, and that they were attacked and killed by Indians in 1798. Now back to Sheriff Sterling."

Bennie joined Charlie and the sheriff again stood at the podium.

"That's pretty much the story. So a mystery that has remained for well over 200 years has now been solved! Talk about a cold case!! We'll now be happy to take your questions."

Barbara Clark with WKYT in Lexington stood and with her cameraman rolling said, "This is simply fascinating! What a story! Two things I would like to ask about are the golden anchor cross and the remains of Seibert's bible. Could we see these?"

"I would have to refer to the State Police to answer about the bible," said the sheriff. "As for the golden anchor cross, it remains with the person that initially discovered the site, and it has been mutually agreed to allow him to remain anonymous."

Bennie stood up at his seat and said, "The charred bible is in no condition to allow anyone to physically handle it. We have it in a sealed bag at Post 10, and if you would like pictures of it just stop by the office and we'll allow that. When we have no future use to hold the bible we'll likely donate it to the Center for Appalachian Research." Dr. Peters nodded his approval with a smile.

Barbara Clark got a frown on her face and said, "It would be VERY interesting to be able to see and take photographs of the cross. Do you think that might be arranged, Sheriff Sterling?"

Bert responded, "Now that we have such a request, I can certainly ask. I just don't know the answer at present. As they say, I'll have to get back to you on that, Ms. Clark."

Barbara Clark nodded, and said, "I sure hope you will. I'll be waiting for your call!".

A.J. Sampson with the Harlan Daily Enterprise stood and asked, "I'll ditto the remarks made by Barbara. I'm certainly going to Post 10 and get pictures of the bible, and to make the story complete we really need to have a photo of the cross. If it could not be arranged to have it physically available, then maybe at least you could take pictures and make them available to us. What do you think Bert?"

"That would seem doable," responded the sheriff. "But again, I'll have to get back to you on it."

Tim Bates with the *Knoxville News-Sentinel* held up his hand as he stood.

"Go right ahead Mr. Bates," said the sheriff.

"This appears to be front page stuff," responded Tim Bates. "There's going to be all kinds of interest in this story. Certainly the solved mystery of the missing pioneers is big news, but I also sense the golden anchor cross to be equally of interest. I'll also second the requests by Barbara and A.J. for more information on it, including photos at the least."

"I understand what you say, and I'll do my best," replied Bert.

"Before we adjourn I would like to again thank each of you for being here, and I want to thank Pastor Bell and Dr. Peters for their assistance. I'll look forward to reading and watching your stories, and hopefully the photos of the bible and the cross will provide you with some additional follow-on stories. I do think the public is going to have a big appetite for this story, I'll be in touch with you as soon as I have something on the cross. Again, thanks for being here."

All the media left. Raymond and Randy walked with Bert and Ape back into the front office and toward the door. They stopped before going out, and the sheriff said, "I think that went good. We managed to get the story out without revealing Carolyn and Kylie. I really don't see a problem with taking photos of the cross and giving them to the media. What do you all think?"

Randy replied, "I think the photos are very important. We're talking here about a very valuable and important piece of history. All we're really certain of is that the cross belonged to Karl Seibert, and that he got it from his father, who got it from his father. That's as far as we can trace it at present. I'm sure Kylie would allow us to further examine the cross if need be, but I just think there's a lot of mystery surrounding that artifact. To provide photos of it to the media would be the correct thing to do, in my opinion."

Pastor Bell responded, "I agree Randy. But it is really important to keep Carolyn and Kylie's names out of the story. They simply would not be safe if it became known that they had possession of the cross. Many people have been hurt, or even killed, for a lot less than $100,000. And it's not just the monetary value ..... I think we'll eventually find out that cross is priceless. We just need to learn more of its history."

"I certainly don't know much about such things," commented Ape. "But I do think we're going down the right path, and I think today's press conference went well. I will be anxious to see what develops when this story hits the news later today."

And with that, all four men said their good-byes to Rosie and headed to their cars for lunch.

27.

Fatso was just about to doze off when the phone rang. He answered it, and listened for several minutes.

"No kidding?" said Fatso. "That's really interesting. I'm sure Pretty Boy will want to hear all about it. I'll tell him you passed it along ..... that'll get you some points."

Fatso hung up the phone and got on the intercom to Pretty Boy. "Just got off the phone. Our snitch at the Harlan Daily Enterprise just called to let me know that the sheriff just completed a most interesting press conference."

Pretty Boy's tobacco streaked face turned white, "Did it have to do with our safe deposit boxes at the bank?"

"No, no," replied Fatso. "You had just told me to keep my ears open for any news from the sheriff's office. So that's what I did. I mentioned to the snitch that he needed to let me know anything that he found out the sheriff was up to. He called to say that A.J. Sampson had just gotten back from a press conference at the sheriff's office and was hot to trot to paste the story on the front page of the Enterprise."

Pretty Boy snarled, "So what the hell is the story Fatso .... quit beating around the bush"

"O.K., O.K.," said Fatso. "You don't have to be so hateful."

"Sorry Fatso, it's just that anything having to do with the sheriff these days makes me a bit jumpy. Can you now tell me what he's up to."

"Sure boss," replied Fatso. "The snitch said that A.J.'s story has to do with the murder of two of Harlan's pioneers. Apparently Indians killed them about 200 years ago."

"So why would that be of interest to me," said Pretty Boy, with the color returning to his face.

"That's not all the story," said Fatso. "It seems that there was a solid gold cross of some kind that was discovered in the remains, and from what A.J. said that cross could be worth major money."

Pretty Boy spit a stream of tobacco juice into his Styrofoam cup and said, "Yeah, but where do we fit in?"

"Well, if we found out who had that cross we might be able to get our hands on it for a big payday," said Fatso.

Pretty Boy thought for a minute, and then said, "True, but likely Sheriff Sterling's got the thing in his evidence room. And I'm sure you remember the tales that Slick told about the monster cat that guards the sheriff's office. But even if the killer cat weren't in the picture, we still couldn't likely lift the thing from the sheriff's office."

Fatso replied, "I see your point, Boss, but I still think it has possibilities."

"I'll agree with you there, Fatso, just keep your ears open and see if you can find out any thing else about it. You never know, we might locate it somewhere that would be easy to hit. Just keep me posted."

"Will do boss." Fatso replied. "Hey boss, what's grey but turns red?"

Silence on the intercom. "An embarrassed elephant."

Pretty Boy slams down the intercom phone. Trigger looks at him and says, "Fatso up to more elephant jokes?"

"How'd you guess," responded Pretty Boy.

Carolyn's mother, Mawie, lived in Wallins about a mile from Maggard's grocery. Mawie's last name was Cottrell. She was in her mid seventies and still very active. Occasionally she liked to walk the distance to Maggard's if she only needed a few groceries. It was good exercise. Today was one of those days she decided to make the trip. It was a beautiful Saturday afternoon, and she hadn't been out of the house for several days.

Fatso saw Mrs. Cottrell walking through the parking lot. She entered the store, and said, "Good afternoon Fatso, I hope the day is going well for you."

"Hi Mrs. Cottrell, good to see you again. Just let me know if I can help you find anything."

"Sure will, Fatso, I just need a couple of things ..... mainly just out for a stroll enjoying the beautiful day and getting some exercise," she said.

Mawie took her time and slowly gathered together the few groceries she intended to get. Finally she took them to the checkout, and pulled out her purse to pay Fatso.

"Mrs. Cottrell, do you know what you call an elephant with a machine gun?" asked Fatso.

Mawie thought for a moment, and then said, "Don't know."

Fatso replied, "You call an elephant with a machine gun, SIR." And both Fatso and Mawie started to giggle.

"That's a good one Fatso, now how much for the groceries?"

"That'll be $6.87 Mrs. Cottrell," said Fatso.

As Mawie handed him her money, Fatso added, "That sure was something about finding the remains of those old pioneers and the golden cross."

Mawie dropped her change on the counter as Fatso handed it to her. "Where did you hear about that?" she asked.

"Sheriff Sterling was talking about it at a press conference this morning," he replied.

"I didn't know it had gone public yet," she said.

"You mean you knew about it already?" he asked.

"Well, yes, I knew about it, since it was my grandson Kylie that found it," she said.

"Well, my, my," said Fatso. "Kylie's going to be one rich little boy."

"I really don't know about that," Mawie replied. "And I probably shouldn't be talking about it. But if the sheriff announced it, I guess it's o.k."

"He still got it?" asked Fatso.

"Oh yes, he keeps it on a chain around his neck all the time. He wouldn't part with it for the world," she said.

"I can sure understand that," replied Fatso, trying hard to keep a big grin off his fat face.

"Well, I must be going Fatso, it was good talking with you," Mawie said as she gathered the bag of groceries and started out the door.

"Yes maim, likewise I'm sure," as the grin spread completely across Fatso's face.

The moment she was out the door Fatso picked up the intercom and buzzed his boss. Pretty Boy answered, "No more elephant jokes!"

"You won't believe what I just found out Pretty Boy," Fatso almost shouted. "That Mrs. Cottrell was just in here buying groceries and I mentioned to her about the sheriff's press conference and what they found, and she said her grandkid was the one that found the gold cross."

"That is interesting, Fatso," said Pretty Boy. "Good work. I'll have to give this some thought."

Pretty Boy hung up the intercom and told Trigger what Fatso had just told him.

"So what we gonna do," asked Trigger.

"Well, first thought was to go after it. But I'm having second thoughts. That cross would be hot as a pistol, and even if we melted it down and sold it for just the price of gold I'm not sure it would be worth the gamble trying to get it from the kid and then trying to sell it. And while the money would be good, that's just not the business we're in. No, after thinking about it, I don't think I want to do anything with it." said Pretty Boy.

"Your call boss," said Trigger, and he got up and started for the door. "I didn't have lunch, think I'll go out and get a bite. Want to go, or you want me to bring you something?"

"No thanks," said Pretty Boy. "Got some stuff I need to do here. See you when you get back."

As Trigger was passing through the grocery store headed for the front door Fatso called to him, "You headed out to get that gold cross from the Potter kid?"

"No," shouted Trigger. "Boss says he don't want no part of it. I'm headed for a late lunch."

"You know why the elephant went into the men's room Trigger," asked Fatso.

No answer. "To see if he could find some nuts," said Fatso as he roared with laughter.

Trigger slammed the front door and left in his car for lunch. Fatso scratched his head and thought to himself, "I don't understand Pretty Boy not wanting that cross, but then I ain't paid to think."

Bad Eye was steaming. He had looked everywhere for the box of trash bags that he was going to use in the robbery. After about an hour of looking everywhere he could think, he finally decided he must have used them.

He walked out the door of the Junk Yard office building and saw Snake walking toward him.

"Just looking for you Snake," Bad Eye said. "I thought I had trash bags for our bank job but I can't find them. I want to get everything all put together as soon as we can. Would you mind running over to Maggard's grocery and getting a box of the heavy duty trash bags?"

"Glad to boss," Snake replied.

"Be careful not to let anyone see you except old Fatso, and tell him you're on your way to Knoxville but needed some trash bags to stow some stuff," Bad Eye said.

"I'm on it, be back shortly," Snake said, and he jumped in the car and took off.

Fatso saw Snake park in the parking lot and start in the grocery. As he entered the door Fatso said, "Well, well, if it ain't old Snake. Thought you'd be in Knoxville by now."

"On my way, Fatso, just needed a box of trash bags to put some junk in," replied Snake.

Snake walked over and saw the trash bags he needed

and picked up a box and walked to the check-out counter to pay.

"Hey Snake, I just heard something real interesting a few minutes ago. I heard that old Sheriff Sterling held a press conference and announced that someone found some old ruins and in the ruins was a gold cross," Fatso said.

"So," said Snake.

"Well, I also learned from Mrs. Cottrell a few minutes ago that the someone that found the gold cross was your son Kylie."

Snake got an interested look on his face and said, "Is that so. Think the cross is worth anything?"

"What I heard is it's worth at least $100,000 just for the gold. Could be worth a hundred times that, depending on what they find out about its history. His grandmother said he always wears it on a chain around his neck. Young Kylie is going to be a rich young man," said Fatso.

"Appreciate your telling me, Fatso," said Snake.

Snake paid for the trash bags and started to leave.

"Hey Snake, you know why the elephants were thrown out of the swimming pool?" asked Fatso.

Snake just looked at him. Fatso said, "Because they couldn't keep their trunks up."

Snake took his trash bags and walked out. Fatso was still laughing after Snake drove off.

Snake thought about the golden cross as he drove back to the Junk Yard. He decided as he drove that he just might sneek back home one night this week and get that golden cross from Kylie. He could get it and not say anything to any of the others at the junk yard, and then have it to take with him to Man-O-War Cay. It would certainly help with his retirement nest egg. The more he thought about it, the better he liked the idea. A big smile formed on his face as he got back to the junk yard.

28.

At about 3:15 Saturday afternoon Sheriff Sterling and Deputy Cornett decided on a coffee break at Creech Cafe.

Ape said, "Sheriff, the word is getting ready to spread about the Seibert ruins. The Enterprise won't carry the story until Monday's paper, since it doesn't do a Sunday issue. But both the Lexington and Knoxville papers will be carrying the story in their Sunday editions. And, of course, it'll be the lead news story on the Lexington television station this evening. When all this happens, I'm a little uneasy about some of our own people as well as strangers trying to uncover similar treasures when they find out the value of that golden cross. It could be like the old California gold rush in 1849."

Bert responded, "Yeah, I'm concerned about that too. But I don't know what to do other than to just wait and see if trouble develops. The only location that has been disclosed to the press is that the ruins were found a few miles from Wallins. So if trouble develops, it's likely to be somewhere in that area."

"Makes sense," said Ape. "I'm also concerned about the follow-on stories that will have pictures of the Seibert bible and the cross. You know how beautiful that cross is, and seeing it's photograph may create even more interest to explore around the area searching for more gold."

"My mother used to tell me not to worry about things I couldn't control," said the sheriff. "I think we just have to try and do what we think is best, and then respond to any thing that develops. I do have to get in touch with Carolyn and Kylie to see if we can get pictures of the cross for the media. I know they won't let it rest until I do."

Fred Knapp walked over and poured more coffee for Bert and Ape. "I heard all about that press conference this morning," Fred said. "Rumors are spreading like wildfire already. Ole Smitty came in around noon and said gold had been discovered in the woods around Wallins, and then I heard several of our regulars say they thought they might be up to a hike in the woods this weekend. Nothing like the smell of money to get people excited."

"They really need to understand that the golden cross that was found was likely the only one ever brought into Harlan County, but of course they probably wouldn't listen," said Bert.

"Yeah," Fred answered. "It's mainly because they don't have anything better to do. They get tired of watching tv, and there's not a lot to do here in downtown Harlan. Not like in the old days." And Fred glanced up at several framed pictures on the wall behind Bert and Ape.

Fred continued, "Those pictures there behind you were all taken in the 1950s in downtown Harlan. The first picture shows one of the four drug stores that people used to visit and hang-out. There was Lee Drug, Howard Drug, Green Miller, and Creech Drug. They all were busy most of the time, and folks enjoyed spending time there. Incidentally, that Creech Drug was owned by some fellow also named Fred, but no relation that I'm aware of. The second picture was taken in front of the VTC bus station, located down on Cumberland Avenue. That was the local bus service. VTC stood for Verda Transportation Company. You could hop on one of the VTC buses and go most anywhere in the county. Course the old Greyhound bus terminal was located across the street from the Post Office on 1st Street. Then the third picture is of the old Harlan swimming pool, located back behind the VTC bus station on Elm Street. Folks used to really enjoy going swimming there during the warm weather. And the 4th and final picture in that series was taken of Belk's Department Store on Central Street. The manager there was called "Wild Bill", and everyone in town loved him.

My point is, all these and many more establishments that thrived at one time in the downtown area are now gone. There's just hardly anything left for people to do."

"Well Fred, I guess that's progress," Ape joked.

Bert pointed at another picture on the wall close to the four Fred had just described, and said, "Fred, that other picture there looks like a lady standing in front of an elevator....what's that all about?"

Fred grinned, and replied, "It doesn't have anything to do with Harlan in the 1950s ... that's for sure, Bert. I really don't know who the lady is or where or when it was taken, but I put it up there just to remind me of the elevator story." Fred chuckled.

"Bet we're getting ready to hear the elevator story," Ape replied.

"It is funny, Ape," Fred said. "Goes like this. An ole Harlan County mountaineer that lived way up in one of our hollers and practically never left home was taken to Knoxville by his son to shop on Gay Street. They went in Millers Department Store to shop, and after a bit the son decided they needed to move up to the 3rd floor to buy something. So the two of them headed for the elevator. The old mountaineer had never even seen an elevator before. He had no idea how they worked. So as they were walking toward the elevator a very elderly lady walked slowly with a cane onto the elevator and it's doors closed. The man and son stood there in front of the elevator doors waiting. The little lights above the doors lit up …. first the 1, then the 2, and finally the 3. And then there was a pause, and the lights again lit up, first 3, then 2, and finally 1. And then the elevator doors opened and the most beautiful young lady you ever laid eyes on walked out of the elevator and across the lobby. The old mountaineer's eyes got big as saucers, and he turned to his son and said, Boy, we got to bring your mother here!"

Bert and Ape joined Fred laughing at the story. Then Bert said, "Fred, that's about all the coffee and Fred tales I can take today. Ape and I got to be going."

As they walked across the street toward the sheriff's office Bert said, "Ape, I'm going to grab my camera from the office and then head over to the Potter's house. Since Snake has taken off to Knoxville, I feel sure Carolyn and Kylie will be home. I'm going to see if they will agree to let me take a picture of that cross. If they agree, I'll take several and then hold them for a day or so before releasing them to the media. No need to get in a hurry."

Ape replied, "O.K. Bert, I'll finish up at the office and then head home. I'm looking forward to a quiet Sunday tomorrow."

"See you Monday, unless something special develops that requires both our attention," said the sheriff. He then picked up his camera, and headed toward Wallins to visit with Carolyn and Kylie Potter.

Bert knocked on the door of the Potter residence, and Kylie showed up quickly to invite him in.

"I just took a chance the two of you would be home," Bert said. "I have something I need to discuss with you."

Carolyn and just finished cooking dinner, and came in and said, "Bert, I've got a pot roast and veggies freshly cooked. How about having dinner with us?"

"Best invitation I've had today," Bert replied. The three of them then headed for the dinning room.

"Hope you won't mind me talking a little business while we eat," said the sheriff.

"Not at all," Carolyn replied.

Kylie asked the Lord's blessing on their meal, and the three then just chatted small talk while they enjoyed their dinner.

Carolyn had fixed a fresh apple pie for desert, and as she started to cut a piece for everyone Bert said, "Other than checking on you two, and enjoying the best home cooked meal I've had in a long time, I did have a little business to discuss. I assumed Snake had headed for Knoxville after the Junk Yard closed down today, and I thought it would work out to come by and talk a bit about things."

"Always happy to talk with you, aren't we Kylie," said Carolyn. Kylie nodded vigorously.

"I held the press conference this morning to disclose the Seibert remains," Bert started. "And I think it went fine. There will be a lot in the newspapers and on television about it over the next few days. I didn't say exactly where the remains were found.....just that they were close to Wallins. And while we did have to disclose the Seibert bible and the golden cross, we did not disclose who found them and were able to keep the two of you anonymous. The reporters did want at least pictures of the two artifacts, and the state police agreed to let them come to their office and take pictures of the charred bible, and I told them that I would need to get permission to photograph the cross."

"That was kind of you Bert," commented Carolyn. "But I know you really didn't have to get our permission. I realize that the cross is actually evidence, and you have gone the extra mile to allow Kylie to keep possession of it. Of course we agree to let you take pictures. Did you bring your camera?"

"Yes, got it right here," said Bert. "But let's finish this delicious apple pie before we start with the pictures!"

After desert Carolyn and Bert had coffee, and Kylie finished his milk. Kylie then stood up and pulled the golden anchor cross from under his shirt. Bert had noticed the bulge in the shirt, and had assumed he was wearing it.

"Kylie every time I see that cross it's beauty just leaves me speechless", said the sheriff.
"I have never encountered anything like it in all my 30 years of police work."

"I just love it," said Kylie. "I have such a special feeling when I wear it. I can't describe the feeling .... it's strange." Carolyn and Bert nodded in agreement.

Bert took the cross from Kylie and sat it on the carpeted floor. He had thought previously that it would be important that the pictures he took did not show anything that could be identified and lead to the Potters. The carpet was a neutral grey, and there was nothing about it that would be associated with the Potter home. He snapped several photographs at various angles and with the cross in different positions. He reviewed the digital photographs, and then showed them to Carolyn and Kylie. Everyone was satisfied.

Bert was putting the camera back in its case when Carolyn said, "When I stopped by mothers to pick up the apples for my apple pie this afternoon, she had just gotten home from a walk to Maggard's grocery. She said she did it just for the exercise .... it was such a pretty day. And as she was checking out with Fatso she said he mentioned your press conference about finding the pioneer's ruins and the golden cross. Mother said she thought that you had announced that Kylie found the cross, and when Fatso asked if she had heard the news she said of course she knew about it because Kylie found it. She didn't know that you did not mention us at the press conference. And she still doesn't know, but I told her I was sure you had not released our names. She apologized, and felt badly about it, but I thought I should tell you."

"Thank you Carolyn," Bert responded. "Fatso must have gotten a call from one of his buddies after the press conference. That news sure did travel fast. I am glad you told me, cause now I know that Pretty Boy and his guys all know that you two have the cross. I don't think they will try anything, they haven't been into robbery so far, but I'll watch them more closely knowing that they know. The bad part is I don't know who else they might tell. I want you and Kylie to be very careful, and sleep with your cell phone and give me a call immediately if you encounter any problems whatever. I can have someone here in a flash."

"That makes me feel lots better, Bert," Carolyn said. Kylie had retrieved the golden cross and put it back under his shirt. He patted it gently.

"You tell Mawie to be very careful when talking to anyone about all this," said Bert. "With all the press coverage it will get for the next several days everyone will be talking about it. She'll just have to take extra caution to not mention the two of you when she talks with people."

"I'll call her tonight and have a good discussion with her about it. I'm sure she won't slip up again," said Carolyn.

Bert walked over to Kylie and rubbed his hair and said, "You two are among my very best friends. I'll be watching things very closely. Thanks for the wonderful meal, and thanks for all the cooperation. Keep in touch." And with that he walked to the door, on to his car, and drove away.

29.

Dr. Randy Peters had driven back to Lexington following the press conference. He always enjoyed the drive. The mountains all around were magnificent, and as he traveled the road his thoughts always went to the early settlers that had traveled the same route in their wagons, on horseback, and on foot. When he reached Pineville, he knew that his journey toward Lexington was along the same route that all those early pioneers had taken after passing through the Cumberland Gap headed West. After reaching Corbin, he then traveled on Interstate 75 to Lexington. All along he thought about the press conference, and wondered how the reporters would present the story. He thought particularly about the golden anchor cross. Although it was discussed in the press conference, he knew that the unusual events that seemed to follow those that possessed the cross were not discussed. To the media the value of the cross seemed to only relate to how much money the cross was worth based on the price of gold. Randy felt certain that the true value of the cross went far, far deeper than the material from which it was formed. He was determined to research this aspect in much more detail.

Randy knew that Barbara Clark would be reporting

the press conference on the evening news. When he got back to Lexington he went immediately to his office to get caught up a bit, and to watch the evening news on his office television at 6 pm. He had arrived back in Lexington around 4 pm, after stopping for a late lunch in London, Kentucky at Weavers Hot Dogs. Weavers had been in business since 1940, and made the best hot dog Randy had ever tasted. He ate two of them. He got comfortable on the couch in his office and tuned in channel 27 at 6 pm.

Late Breaking News, came across the tv screen, followed by a close up of Barbara Clark who then said, *"This morning there was a press conference in Harlan conducted by Sheriff J. Bert Sterling that dealt with a most interesting subject. The sheriff reported that someone walking in the woods near the small town of Wallins, which is about 10 miles from Harlan, came across the ruins and skeletons of what were determined to be those of two early pioneers on their way to Harlan in 1798. The Kentucky State Police examined the skeletons and ruins and confirmed the identity of the two persons to be Reverend Karl Seibert and his wife Mary . They were in route to Harlan to establish a church when apparently attacked by Indians who killed them and set their wagon on fire. Two artifacts that were found in the ruins included a charred bible, which the State Police said contained Reverend Seibert's name, and a beautiful golden anchor cross.*

Now on the screen you see a picture of the bible, which the State Police allowed us to photograph. As you can see, it is very fragile and largely burned from the fire. The golden cross remains in the possession of the anonymous person that found it. From its description it is estimated to be worth at least $100,000. Sheriff Sterling promised to produce photographs of it shortly. We were briefed at the conference by Dr. Randy Peters, Director of U.K.'s Center for Appalachian Research, about the history associated with the settling of Harlan, which was first called Mount Pleasant. It had been first settled by a Samuel Howard in 1796. Howard and Seibert had become friends while the two of them lived in Williamsburg, Virginia prior to Howard's establishing the settlement of Mount Pleasant. It was Howard who then wrote to Reverend Seibert requesting him to come and establish a church in what is now Harlan. The last Samuel Howard or anyone else ever heard from the Seiberts was in a letter that Reverend Seibert mailed to Howard from Williamsburg saying he and his new bride Mary were leaving for Mount Pleasant to establish a church there. Nothing more was known about them until the discovery of their ruins near Wallins, well over 200 years later. I'll keep you posted on this late breaking story. Stay tuned to Channel 27. Barbara Clark reporting."

Randy turned the television off, and sat back on the sofa and thought about what was just aired.

30.

Sheriff Sterling lived in a home in the subdivision of Sunny Acres in Harlan. His house was only a couple of blocks from the Post 10 Kentucky State Police offices. On his way home Saturday evening he stopped by to take a look at Reverend Seibert's bible. It was indeed in extremely delicate condition, but he could make out traces of handwriting on the page showing in the zip locked bag. By knowing that the name was Karl Seibert he was able to discern the inscription. He thanked the officer for showing him the bible, and then headed home for the evening.

Sunday morning Bert always got up early, leaving plenty of time to drink coffee and read the papers before going to church. This morning he was particularly anxious to see the papers. He received both the Lexington Herald-Leader and Knoxville News Sentinel. Through the week he also received the Harlan Daily Enterprise, not published on Sundays. After starting his coffeemaker, Bert walked to his front lawn to retrieve the two newspapers. He brought them inside and got comfortable in a chair at his kitchen table, spreading the newspapers out on the table.

The headlines read:

In the Lexington paper:

**_Skeletons and Remains of Early Pioneers
Found in Harlan_**

And in the Knoxville paper:

**_Gold and a Bible Belonging to 1798 Harlan County
Pioneers Discovered
Skeletons Reveal They Were Murdered by Indians_**

He then read the articles in both papers. They each reported pretty much exactly what was discussed at the press conference. He felt relieved that there was nothing in either paper that greatly embellished or added untrue facts to the story. It was good reporting. He had heard Barbara Clark's account on television last night, and was equally pleased with it. But he did know he would have to send them all the photographs of the cross, but that could wait until tomorrow. He drank two cups of coffee and then started to get ready for church.

At the end of the service, Pastor Raymond Bell stood on the steps of the New Hope Baptist Church and greeted and thanked each who attended. When Carolyn and Kylie shook his hand he whispered to them that if they had a few minutes he would like to see them in his study. They indicated they would be happy to meet with him. A few moments later Sheriff Sterling was greeted by Pastor Bell, and Raymond again whispered the same request to him. He also said he would be glad to meet. After greeting all his parishioners, Pastor Bell quickly headed for his study.

When he arrived he hugged all three of his friends and asked them to please be seated. Then the pastor took his seat behind his desk.

"I know you've all read the papers and watched the television report about the Seibert findings," Raymond said. "I was pleased with them, and I hope you were as well." Carolyn, Kylie, and the sheriff all slowly nodded affirmatively.

The pastor continued, "The one thing that was not in any of those reports has to do with the unusual events that seem to happen to anyone having the cross. Now I realize we did not say anything about these to the reporters, but I have some concerns, and just wanted to bounce these off you. Sooner or later these stories about the cross will get out. When they do, we need to have our ducks in a row as to how to handle them. Later last night I called Dr. Peters and discussed this with him, and he was in agreement. He said he would dig deeper into the history of the anchor cross and try and find some answers. I don't know how successful he will be, but I'm certainly glad he's going to make a search. Frankly, I think the answers are to be found in the religious representation of the cross. The more I've thought about the events that we know have occurred, it just would seem that the combination of the sign of the cross and the words pax tecum on the cross, that mean 'peace be with you', must be significant parts to the puzzle. Both Randy and myself will continue to search for answers, but in the meantime I'm concerned that if any of these stories emerge we need to be ready with a response. What do you think?"

Bert spoke up, "I do understand what you say, pastor. But frankly I'm just not too concerned about this. The stories you refer to would only surface from someone doing in depth research into the diary of Samuel Howard, or the ancestry of Karl Seibert, or hear them from one of us in this room. None of these will likely occur. Of course, Randy knows about these, but certainly he will not be publicizing them. So I think all we can do is to continue to look into them, and if someone does find out and ask about them, I think we can only say we just don't have a good understanding. Agreed?"

Everyone said yes, and stood. Pastor Bell thanked each of them, again gave hugs, and they all left for home.

It was Sunday evening and Snake had gotten more and more excited about the possibility of stealing the golden cross from his son Kylie. He knew he needed to work fast because Bad Eye would be closely riding heard on everyone next week in getting all set up for the bank robbery on Friday. He had given lots of thought as to how he could get the cross without anyone knowing, and he had devised a plan that involved his going to the house tonight, slipping in with his door key, and going to Kylie's bedroom and use chloroform to render his son unconscious while he removed the golden cross from around his neck. After that, he would simply slip back out of the house and return to the junk yard without being noticed. Seemed like a perfect plan to him. He would slip out of the junk yard after dinner. Bad Eye, Jones, and Billie usually got drunk soon after eating, and Snake usually joined them, but tonight he'd say he didn't feel good and go to his bunk. When the other three had passed out, he would leave to get the cross.

One problem was that he did not have any chloroform. He really didn't want to hurt his son, so he didn't want to knock him out. And he didn't want his son to identify him.....that would spoil everything. So the best thing he could come up with was to get some chloroform and while Kylie was sleeping he would slip in and hold a rag saturated with the chloroform on his face until he passed out. That way he wouldn't see who was doing it, and by holding the cloth on his face he wouldn't be able to make any noise before becoming unconscious. But he had to get a bottle of chloroform. Fortunately for him, he knew a fellow crook in Harlan that specialized in robbing people by using chloroform. He called him on his cell and said he would give him $100 if he would bring a bottle of it to the junk yard gate on Saturday night at midnight. He told him he would meet him there, and that if he told anyone about it he would greatly shorten his life. His friend agreed.

Snake thought Sunday night would be a good time to easily get into his house without disturbing Carolyn. She had to work on Monday, and always went to bed early. Kylie always retired then too. So Snake figured that if he left the junk yard around 11 pm, and by that time all three of his friends would certainly be passed out drunk, he would have little problem in getting to the house, slipping to Kylie's bedroom, drugging him with the chloroform, grabbing the cross, and getting back to the junk yard. He figured by midnight he'd be sleeping at the junk yard with a golden cross worth at least $100,000. That would be a substantial boost to his retirement income.

All went just as planned on Sunday after dinner. Bad Eye, Jones, and Billie got dead drunk and passed out by 10 o'clock. Snake quietly waited until shortly before 11, and then took off. He parked about a quarter mile from the house, and walked from there. He felt fortunate that Carolyn and Kylie didn't have a dog ..... barking could have been a big problem. He quietly stepped to the door, unlocked it, and walked into his house. All was quiet. Visibility was good enough from night lights that Carolyn had placed all over the house to allow him to see clearly where he was going. Carolyn slept in the main bedroom downstairs. Kylie's bedroom was one of two that were upstairs. After reaching the top of the stairs, Snake uncorked the chloroform and poured a good dose in a large rag he had brought with him. He then proceeded to sneak into Kylie's room. Kylie was sound asleep. Snake thought he could hear him snoring lightly. He was lying on his back, so his face was in a position that would be easy to place the rag over. Snake also noticed a large bulge in Kylie's pajama top. He was sure the bulge was his prize!

He quietly slipped beside the bed, and then quickly placed the chloroform soaked rag over Kylie's face. He struggled, and tried to scream, but Snake was able to apply enough pressure to keep any sound from escaping. The sweet smell of the chloroform filled the room. After a minute or so, Kylie succumbed to the anesthetic and went limp. Snake continued to keep the rag on his face for another minute or so, then removed it and tossed it in a trash container beside the bed. Then he reached for Kylie's neck. His fingers slipped around the loop of the leather necklace that held the golden anchor cross. He then carefully lifted the necklace over Kylie's head, with the golden cross hanging on the bottom of it. As he was removing it he could see clearly from the night light how very beautiful it was, and he was certain it had to be pure gold and would be worth a mint.

He held the necklace with his left hand, and stood up beside the bed. He then took his right hand and wrapped his fingers tightly around the golden anchor cross. The pain was something he had never felt before. It was all he could possibly do to not shout or scream. He dared not wake Carolyn. But when he looked at his right hand he could see smoke coming from it. The cross was literally burning into the flesh of his right hand. He thought he could even see bone from one of the fingers on his right hand. He immediately turned his hand over and violently shook it to disengage the cross from the flesh. The cross fell onto the bed. Snake went as quietly as possible down the stairs and out the door. Amazingly, his hand did not hurt. The burns were so severe that all the nerves in his hand were numb. He hurried along the road to his car, got in, and managed to get the car started using his left hand. By midnight he was back in his bunk at the junk yard, but the golden anchor cross was not with him.

31.

At about 3 am on Monday morning Kylie woke up with a bad headache. He first thought he would go down and tell his mother that he didn't feel well, but then he thought she really needed her sleep in order to work on Monday, so he stayed in bed and thought. It seemed like he had a terrible dream, like he couldn't breathe and something was pressing on his face. But he couldn't remember. Then he realized that the bulge in his pajama top was missing and he felt around to see if the cross had shifted over to his side, but he didn't feel it. Then he felt for its leather necklace around his neck, but it wasn't there. He started to panic. Where was his beautiful golden anchor cross? He raised up in bed to look around, thinking it could have come off during his dream, and was greatly relieved when he saw the cross laying toward the foot of his bed. It wasn't lost, it was there! He reached down and picked it up, and noticed some funny looking specks attached to it ..... they looked dark. He couldn't imagine what they might be. He decided to get up and take his cross to the bathroom and inspect it closer. In the bathroom he turned on the light and looked at the cross. The spots seemed to be in several places, and looked a bit like little pieces of burned paper or something. He decided he'd wash them off, and turned on the water in the sink and let the water run over it. The spots seemed to disappear. He turned the water off and reached for a towel and dried the cross. It looked to be back good as new. Kylie was now satisfied, and happy, and placed the leather necklace back around his neck and gently placed the cross under his pajama top. He was greatly relieved to have his cross back, and glad too that he didn't have to wake his mother. He went back to bed and got under the covers. He still had his headache, but that would just have to wait till morning, and it might even be gone by then. Once again he thought about his bad dream, and decided he would tell his mother about it in the morning also.

Carolyn usually got up at 6 am on a work day. Her alarm went off, and she popped up and went into the bathroom for her shower. After the shower, she threw on a robe and went into the kitchen to start to prepare breakfast for her and Kylie. Usually Kylie would hear her in the kitchen and come down in his pajamas ready for breakfast. He always took his shower in the evenings before bed. After a few minutes Kylie walked into the kitchen and said, "Morning Mom, I've got a headache."

"Oh dear, I'm so sorry. I'll get you something for it," and she left for the medicine cabinet in her bathroom. She returned shortly, got a glass of water, and gave it to Kylie with the tablets.

"Thanks Mom," Kylie said after taking the medicine.

"You're welcome buddy," Carolyn replied. "Now you eat your toast and cereal and drink your milk. Then you should maybe lie down on the sofa until I get dressed and we're ready to take you to Mawies. Hopefully that headache will go away."

"O.K.," Kylie responded. "But I wanted to tell you that I had a bad dream last night too. I dreamed that there was something pressing on my face, and something smelled funny, and then I woke up with my headache. And I must have lost my cross during the dream, because I found it at the foot of my bed after I woke up. It was really a funny dream."

Carolyn looked a bit puzzled, and then patted Kylie on the head. "Well, the important thing is that everything seems o.k. now, except for the headache. We'll talk more about it on the way to Mawies. I've got to run upstairs now and make your bed and then finish getting ready. You finish up breakfast, get dressed, and then rest on the sofa till I'm ready."

"O.K. mom," replied Kylie.

Carolyn rushed upstairs to make Kylie's bed, and as she was doing so she noticed a strange rag in Kylie's trash can beside his bed. She reached down and picked it up, and the sweet smell of chloroform just about knocked her over. She was stunned. She knew Kylie had nothing to do with that rag, and the very strong odor clearly indicated it had been placed in the trash can recently. It was at that moment that she realized that Kylie's dream was likely not a dream at all, but rather someone had managed to get into their home and attempted to steal Kylies golden anchor cross. It didn't require a detective to put those facts together. She decided she would get dressed, get Kylie to Mawies, and then call Sheriff Sterling on her way to work.

32

It was just shortly after 8 am and Sheriff Sterling and Deputy Cornett had first checked in at the office with Rosie, and learned nothing required their immediate attention, so they walked across the street to Creech Cafe for coffee. When they walked in they missed hearing Polly greet them, and didn't see her around. They took a seat on stools at the counter and waited on Fred to get to them. A couple of minutes later Fred appeared with coffee and poured two steaming cups.

"Morning Fred," Bert said. "We missed Polly..... where's the ole bird?"

Fred replied, "Polly wasn't eating right, and I took her to the vet on Saturday. She said she needed to keep her for a couple of days to observe and run some tests. I'll pick her up after work today. I'll tell her you two said you missed her, that'll cheer her up."

"You do that Fred," Ape commented.

"You know the ole bird's getting some age on her .... I sure would hate to lose her," Fred said. Losing a pet can be almost as bad as losing a friend or relative. I'm reminded of the passing recently of our fine Harlan native son that became a U.S. Federal Judge. I was greatly impressed by the nice article of tribute that a good friend of his wrote for the Enterprise."

Fred walked toward the back of the cafe and pulled a large framed article from one of his walls and brought it back to the counter and laid it in front of the sheriff and deputy. "Don't know if you read this, but take a look and tell me what you think."

Karl

Most folks named Carl spell it with a "C". Two that were especially important to me and my life were Karl's with a "K"; Karl Otto Lange and Karl Forester. I wanted to share some of my memories about my dear lifelong friend Karl Forester.

The two of us grew up together in Harlan, Kentucky. My earliest memories of Karl involved playing together with him when we were around kindergarten age. We lived on the same block in Harlan, and at that age we liked to ride "scooters". These were very simple devices that kids at that time usually rode prior to being old enough for bicycles. I recall many times going up to Karl's home very early in the morning and pecking on his bedroom window to wake him up so that the two of us could ride our scooters all around the neighborhood. As we grew a bit older we "graduated" to bicycles, and had many grand times riding those together.

We played together daily. I still remember his phone number (1443W, my number was 1393) because I called it several times daily to talk. As with all kids, we did have some disagreements. I remember one occasion where we had been playing together and had some kind of disagreement and decided to part company. We were in the alley between Karl's home and my home, and when we left to go our respective directions Karl had his back to me and I picked up a rock and lobbed it into the air in Karl's direction. As luck would have it, it hit Karl smack on the top of his head, at which point he let out a shrill scream and started running home to tell his mother. Needless to say, when I reached my home my mother was waiting with a "switch" to give me a good one.

Karl and I also liked to earn money. Karl's home was located on Clover Street on a corner lot, next to what was then called the "Teacher's Club", which was a building owned by the school system but not used for classes. Karl and I would purchase candy wholesale and set up a table at the corner of his house lot and sell the candy bars to those passing on the sidewalk. We actually did pretty good at this, supplementing our spending money.

Karl's father Bill owned a men's clothing store in Harlan called "Forester and Spillman". When we were young kids Forester and Spillman was located in the greyhound bus building across from the post office on 1st street. The business had a storage room in the basement of the building, and Karl and I decided we would "publish" a newspaper called the "Harlan Daily Press". To do this we took a portable typewriter to the storage room and pecked out "news" on one sheet of paper with about 4 carbon copies. Because we did not have duplicating machines, we had to repeat typing the one page "newspaper" with its 4 carbon copies several times in order to produce the 20 or so copies that we sold on the streets of Harlan for 5 cents each. Of course what we perceived as "news" was little more than family events, and some were a bit embarrassing to family members. One story I recall was when we reported that my Uncle Estil Giles had taken a trip in his new "Buck" (what we meant was "Buick", but we had lots of spelling failures!).

Karl and I were huge UK football and basketball fans. Of course when we were kids there was no television, and we listened to most every game on the radio. When we reached about our first year in High School, our parents agreed to let us ride the bus the Lexington, to stay in the Phoenix Hotel, and to go to a UK ball game. Looking back on this now, it seems impossible that they would have agreed to such a thing, but they did. I recall that Karl and I got our room in the Phoenix Hotel, and then thinking we were such "big stuff" we decided we needed to get a bottled beverage. Since I was a big kid, I was elected to go to the liquor store to get a bottle of wine. I did, and purchased a bottle of Mogen David wine. We put it in *ice in our hotel room and decided we would open it to celebrate Kentucky's victory after the game. When we arrived back in our hotel room after the game we found that the maid had been there and about half our bottle of wine was gone!!*

Karl and I loved to play games. We had one game that consisted of a rectangular box that had an electric light bulb in it. The game came with a bunch of "plays" that were sheets of thick paper. There were "offensive" and "defensive" plays, and each player would select one, and then these would be placed together and laid on top of the light box and then a slide pulled gradually out to reveal the results of the selected play. Karl and I had little cards, sort of like baseball cards, that had pro football players on them and we would each have a complete set of these cards for our different teams. We would set out these cards beside the game box and thus supplement the game by having teams and players involved. We played these games for many, many hours on end.

A few years later, when Karl and I had just gotten our driver's licenses, I remember visiting again with Karl at his Elm Street home. I was driving my 1949 Chevrolet that I had worked one summer to purchase for $300. Unfortunately, Karl and I were always looking for gas money for our cars. This particular day we needed gas money for my car and Karl suggested that we load up his mother's clothes washer and take it to the junk yard and *sell it for scrap for gas money. Keep in mind that this was a perfectly good washing machine! But sell it for scrap we did, and I do remember that Karl was grounded for many weeks thereafter!*

One year when we were in High School Karl and I had gotten mad at each other over something and had not spoken to each other for several days. There was a Harlan High School football game in Middlesboro and I drove there with several friends in my 1949 Chevy, and Karl drove there with one of his friends in his parents Plymouth. After the game, we both left driving back to Harlan. It was raining. I came upon Karl about half way to Pineville. The road between Middlesboro and Pineville was of the "three lane" type, whereby you could pass going uphills. I pulled up beside Karl going up a hill, and when he saw it was me he put his Plymouth accelerator to the floor. And, of course, I put my Chevy accelerator to the floor. I remember seeing 96 miles per hour on my speedometer as I just passed Karl at the top of a long hill and started to pull in front of him. As I turned I could feel my car starting to slip on the wet road. Coming up the hill right in front of me in the opposite direction was a large gas truck!! I barely got my car in front of Karl's as the gas truck passed by. I always thought that the very large kid in the center of the back seat of my car was the only thing that kept my car from sliding into the gas truck. Later that year after Karl and I were once again on friendly terms we were talking about this race. I admitted to Karl that my hands and arms were shaking so much that I had to pull over and rest after our race. Karl admitted that he had to do the same.

I fondly recall the summer in High School that I worked for my Uncle Henry Giles in his ready-mixed concrete business. I would work about 12 hours per day.....it didn't get dark in the summer until after 8 pm. Almost every day after work I would come home, shower, and dress and Karl would come by and pick me up and we would go to the Harlan Drive-In restaurants to visit with the other high school kids. There were 5 drive-in restaurants in Harlan, and we would go from one to the other visiting with friends at each.

Karl's father Bill had moved his store from the bus building on 1st street to the corner of Central and Main, across the street from Howard Drug. Karl's dad really took great interest in Karl's grades in High School. I recall walking into Forester and Spillman one day with Karl when we had just received our report cards. Karl's dad knew that it was report card day, and as soon as we walked into the store he asked Karl for his report card. Karl showed it to him, reluctantly......Karl and gotten one bad grade. I recall Bill's face growing very red as he looked at the report card, after which he said to Karl "This makes my butt crave buttermilk". I never did know what that meant, but I always thought it was funny. Karl, not so much so.

When it came time to go to college there was never a

question about where to go for Karl or for me. UK was the only choice. We had been such big UK sports fans, that the choice of college only meant UK. So in September, 1958 Karl and his father and me and my father loaded up the car and headed for Lexington. Karl and I were room mates in 106 Donovan Hall. I recall so well our parking the car beside the dorm and unloading all our gear into 106.

After our freshman year, we moved together to a rooming house on Linden Walk. And then later, we roomed together in another rooming house on Transylvania Park. One story I recall vividly during this time involved Karl having a date (don't recall if this was Tracy or before he met her) and wanted to borrow my car, since he did not have one at that time. I agreed, and Karl was out late that night and came in and left the keys on my desk. Myself and a couple other guys that were rooming at the house decided we would play a prank on Karl. The car that I had was one of those where you could take the keys out of the ignition and leave the car running (unheard of today). So the next morning we went out and started my car, left the motor running, took the keys out and locked the doors, and went back inside the house and laid the keys back on my desk where Karl had left them. Karl was still asleep, so we woke him and said we needed to leave shortly for class. Karl got ready and we all walked outside the house and then saw my car parked in front of the house locked with the motor running! I looked at Karl and said, "My lord Karl, you left the motor running last night when you got in!". Karl got a terrible look on his face and started immediately with the apologies. I don't think he ever figured out that we had pulled that prank!

Another remembrance I have of Karl about that time was when we were rooming together on Linden Walk the television series Bonanza was very popular. It aired on Saturday night, and only one person, a fellow named Don Pierson, had a television. Don was a graduate student in Psychology, and looked after the house for the owner. Every Saturday evening Karl and I along with several other of those rooming there would gather in Don's room to watch Bonanza. It was a special treat that everyone looked forward to each week.

When we were Juniors at UK Karl joined a fraternity. He then moved to live in the frat house and he and I lost close contact with each other for a few years. Karl and Tracy were married along about this time, and I can recall visiting them in their apartment on North Broadway. After graduating from UK with a history major, Karl and Tacy moved to Harlan and Karl started teaching school in Loyall. It was then that Harlan lawyer Gene Goss, one of Karl's cousins, talked Karl into going back to Law School at UK, and then joining him in his practice in Harlan.....doing a lot of "black lung" litigation. During this period of time I did not have close contact with Karl, just occasionally seeing him and Tracy when I visited Harlan.

I think it was 1988 when Karl was appointed a U.S.

Federal Judge by Ronald Reagan, and Karl moved his family back to Lexington. I knew very little of his activities as a Federal Judge, other than what I read in the papers. Karl and I always got together at least twice a year, once on March 30th, my birthday, and again on May 2, Karl's birthday. Karl would always come over to UK to pick me up and take me out for a birthday luncheon on my birthday, and I would do the same for him on May 2. We did that for many, many years. Other than that, we would often see each other at reunions and various other get togethers.

Today, March 29th, 2014 I had planned to pick up a lunch for Karl, Tracy, and myself and take it to his home to celebrate my birthday tomorrow. My wife Carolyn and myself had just gotten back from spending the winter in Florida, and I had called and talked with Karl just about a week ago about the birthday luncheon at his home. I knew, of course, that Karl was suffering from Cancer and that he was unable to get out, and wanted to not break our chain of birthday luncheons. Karl readily agreed to the plan, and said he would look forward greatly to seeing me and having our usual birthday lunch on March 29th.

Tracy called me this morning at about 9:00 am to say that Karl was non responsive and therefore would have to cancel our luncheon today. I was so sad to hear the news. Further, she said that they were just waiting for the end. And then, at about 2 pm today Karl's good friend Jack Sterling called me to say that a friend of Karl's in Harlan had called him to say that Karl had passed later this morning.

I will always remember Karl with not only the few sample stories related above, but with hundreds of others that we shared together for 74 years. I will greatly miss Karl.

Dick Edwards, 3/29/2014

Bert and Ape both finished reading the article at the same time. Bert said, "Yeah, you can certainly feel the lifelong friendship and the loss in that article. Always very sad when we lose friends. I guess the important thing is to make sure we know where we're going when we reach our end on this earth, and to try and make the most of the time we are granted. We never know when it will end .... got to be ready."

Ape nodded and said, "Very true. And I do hope Polly gets a clean bill of health Fred"

Fred filled up Bert and Ape's cups, and then turned to walk off just as Bert's cell phone rang.

"Oh, Hi Carolyn, everything O.K.?"

"Oh boy, I'll need to talk with you. Ape and I were just finishing coffee here with Fred. I'll walk down to the bank and we can talk there if you can spare a few minutes. See you shortly."

"Carolyn Potter?" asked Ape.

"Yeah, and it sounded like something happened last night to Kylie. He's fine now, but I need to run down and talk with her. You go on to the office and I'll see you soon as I get through talking to Carolyn at the bank."

"Fine....see you in a bit," replied Ape.
The two walked out of Creech Cafe, Ape headed for the office and Bert headed for the bank.

As soon as Bert walked into Miners Bank Carolyn waved to him and indicated he should join her in Calvin Brown's office. Calvin had left going to the post office and told Carolyn to use his office to meet with the sheriff. Bert gave her a hug and told her to sit and tell him what happened to Kylie.

Carolyn related what had happened that morning at home, and told him what she suspected happened last night based on the chloroform rag she found in Kylie's trash can.

"Sure seems to add up that someone tried to steal that cross," said the sheriff. "I don't understand why they didn't get it, but I'm sure thankful they didn't. You got any idea who it might have been?"

"Unfortunately I do," Carolyn replied. "Whoever it was entered the house without making any noise. All the windows and doors were locked this morning....no sign of entry. It would seem that they entered with a key. Other than Mawie, Snake is the only one I know with a key."

"Yeah, I hear you, but he's supposed to be in Knoxville isn't he?" asked Bert.
"That's what he said, but I haven't heard anything from him.....I just don't know for sure."

Bert thought for a moment, and then said, "Well, thank the good Lord everything turned out O.K. I'll keep an eye out for Snake, and try and do some inquiring about his whereabouts. In the meantime, if anything at all happens that seems suspicious you give me a call. Now get back to work and try not to think about last night. I'm sure it'll be O.K."

Carolyn stood and gave Bert a hug. Bert then left and Carolyn returned to her teller's window.

33.

Bad Eye and the boys slept late on Monday morning. The night before all but Snake had consumed far too much moonshine and they needed their rest. Snake had another problem. His right hand had started to swell as he drove home last night, and by the time he made it back to the junk yard he knew he had to get something for it. Fortunately for him, the junk yard was required by law to have a large and well equipped first aid kit. He opened it, treated his wound as best he could, and then bandaged his hand. It did start to feel a bit better, and he was so tired he fell off to sleep, and didn't awaken until he heard Bad Eye saying, "You all get your fat asses out of bed, we'll got things to do!"

Jones & Billie took about 15 minutes to finally put their feet on the floor, and Snake lay with his hands under the cover thinking of the story to tell Bad Eye about how he got burned. Finally Bad Eye came over to his bunk and reached down and jerked his covers off.

"What's all that bandage on your hand Snake?"

"Well Bad Eye, after you boys got too drunk to help me last night, I went out to work on my pickup truck. Had a muffler leak, so I let it warm up real good so I could hear the leak properly, and when I got all in position under the truck to wrap duct tape around the hole in the exhaust pipe I stuck my right hand up between the pipe and the manifold. I had my left hand holding the pipe a little further down and I guess I pulled too hard on it and the hanger broke. The pipe then swung down and forward and pinned my right hand between the hot manifold and the exhaust pipe. Worst damn burn I ever got. I bandaged it up using our first aid kit, but it still hurts."

"Well hell's bells," said Bad Eye. "Like we ain't got enough problems. It's just lucky you're left handed, but all that bandage on your right hand certainly ain't going to help in the robbery. You can still handle a gun with your good left hand, but you won't be able to do nothing with that right paw."

Jones and Billie both giggled, and Billie said, "Guess we'll just call you lefty!"

Bad Eye said, "It ain't funny, and it could cause us big problems. But we'll just have to deal with it. You all get yourselves dressed and ready for breakfast, and then we'll start rehearsing our plan for Friday. We're burning daylight!"

The sheriff had walked back to his office from Miners Bank. As he walked in the door he automatically reached up and gave a good pet to Preacher Puss. She purred loudly, and then bounced down, first onto Ape's desk and then to the floor, and followed the sheriff as he headed back toward his office. She rubbed gently against his right ankle.

"Rosie, I'm back. Everything quiet?" Bert asked.

"Yep, all's good at the moment. Ape took off to answer a call from a guy at Loyall that apparently got a tire slashed on his car last night. He should be back shortly," responded Rosie.

"I'm getting ready to send out the pictures of the Seibert golden anchor cross to the media. I promised at the press conference I'd try and do that. I'll try putting everything together on my computer and then get you to take a look at it before I send it. Shouldn't take too long," Bert said.

"Oh, great! I'm dying to see the pictures. I've heard about it from Ape, but I just can't imagine what it looks like," Rosie replied. "And to just think that it was actually carried by one of the very first pioneers into Harlan County!"

"It is a treasure," Bert replied, and he closed his office door behind him.

Bert took the digital storage card from his camera and inserted it into his computer and retrieved and stored the pictures he had taken of the golden cross. He looked at his computer screen at one of the pictures. How beautiful! Although the pictures didn't really do the cross justice, they still were able to convey it's beauty. Bert attached all the photos he had taken to the email addressed to each of the media persons present at the press conference, and composed the following message to accompany them:

Attached please find photographs of the golden anchor cross that was found in the ruins of the wagon brought to Harlan County in 1798 by Reverend Karl Seibert and his wife Mary. The cross is approximately 4 inches wide, 6 inches tall, and about one half inch thick. It has the Latin words pax tecum inscribed on the horizontal arm. These can be interpreted as meaning "Peace be with you". The cross remains the property of the person who found it, and that person wishes to remain anonymous. Currently Dr. Randy Peters, Director of the University of Kentucky's Center for Appalachian Research, is searching to try and determine additional information about the cross. Such information will be shared with you if and when I receive it.

Thank you,
J. Bert Sterling, Sheriff of Harlan County

Bert punched the intercom button for Rosie. "Got it ready for your inspection," he said.

Rosie bounced in the sheriff's office and came around to his side to look at the press release on his computer. She read it, and then she looked at the attached photographs.

"That cross is beautiful beyond description!! When the public sees these pictures I've got a feeling we'll be getting a lot more calls wanting additional information," she said.

"I'm sure that's true, Rosie," Bert replied. "You see anything that I should change, or any other suggestion before I send it?"

"No," she replied. "I think it's good to go."

Rosie turned and went back into the front office, and Bert hit the "send" key on his computer.

34.

Dr. Randy Peters had gotten started researching further the Seibert golden anchor cross on Saturday evening after watching Barbara Clark's 6 pm evening news telecast.

He first obtained the copy of Samuel Howard's diary from the archives in his Center for Appalachian Research, and reviewed the sections where Howard made reference to his friend Karl Seibert and his golden cross. By carefully studying the diary he was able to establish the following that had been written about the cross:

1) The cross had been passed down in Karl Seibert's family as far back as Karl's great grandfather. There was no reference in the diary as to how Karl's great grandfather came to receive the cross.

2) Howard was told by Seibert that his father had given him the cross just before he started the journey from Bremerhaven, Germany to Virginia.

3) It was recorded that Karl had stated that he had heard stories of how his father and grandfather had encountered assistance that defied explanation while wearing the cross.

4) There was a story told to Howard by Seibert about how while wearing the cross he fell off a 100 yard cliff overlooking the James River without being injured.

5) While wearing the cross Karl had a vision that affirmed his trip to Harlan.

Randy was also aware of Kylie's experience wearing the cross when Snake attempted to strike Carolyn with the baseball bat which unexplainably bounced and hit his father rendering him unconscious.

Given this information, Randy then wanted to try and trace the origin of the cross. To do this he needed to know more information about Karl Seibert's great grandfather, since it seemed that he had obtained the cross from some source outside the Seibert family. One of Randy's favorite hobbies was genealogy, and he was very expert at tracing the lineage of people on the internet. He sat down at his computer and worked for the next 3 hours establishing the ancestors of Reverend Karl Seibert of

Bremerhaven, Germany. He finally found that his great grandfather on his father's side of the family was one Reverend Otto Seibert who lived for the majority of his life in Southern Germany at Munich.

Randy then used his computer to get a biography of Reverend Otto Seibert. He learned he was born in 1670 and after establishing a church in Munich had become good friends with a Catholic Bishop there. In the biography, it further stated that there was an occasion where Rev. Seibert had performed an act that saved the Bishop from great bodily harm, and the Bishop had presented to him a gift of a golden anchor cross that he had received from Pope Clement XI. The cross had a name, it was called the Savior's Cross.

Randy then started to research the Savior's Cross on his computer. What he found was astounding. There was more than one of these crosses. Apparently when the Roman Emperor Constantine the Great ruled from 306 to 337 AD he was able to obtain from Pope Sylvester I a gold bar that was thought to date back to the time of Christ. It was one of a group of gold bars, called St. Peter's Gold, that were thought to have been blessed by Christ and passed to St. Peter, the First Bishop of Rome, and the first Pope, to be used to help establish the church. It was said that some of these very bars were still in the church at the time of Pope Sylvester I, from 314 to 335

AD. Emperor Constantine was the first Roman emperor to claim conversion to Christianity. He also introduced a new gold coin, the solidus, to help combat inflation. It was the combination of these two things, his conversion to Christianity and his familiarity with melting and forming gold, that led him to ask Pope Sylvester I to allow him to use one of the St. Peter's gold bars to produce an anchor cross that he had envisioned in a dream. Up until the time of Constantine the anchor was the primary symbol associated with Christianity. Constantine was determined to make the cross as the primary symbol, and so it has been since about 325 AD. His vision was to combine these two Christian symbols into one, and call it the Savior's Cross. Pope Sylvester I agreed to Constantine's request, and 6 of the beautiful golden anchor crosses, then called the Savior's Cross, were produced from one bar of St. Peter's Gold. Constantine kept one of these, and the other 5 were given to Pope Sylvester I. These 5 were then passed down from Pope to Pope, and for reasons unknown, Pope Clement XI in about 1710 gave one of these crosses to the Bishop from Munich, who then gave the cross as a gift to Reverend Otto Seibert a few years later.

Randy looked at his watch, it was 4 am on Sunday morning! He was very tired, but extremely pleased with his research. From all he could understand, the anchor cross that Karl Seibert brought to Harlan was the very cross that was given to his great grandfather, Otto Seibert, and the gold from which it had been made had been blessed by Christ. Wow!

After writing up the findings on his computer, Randy locked up shop and headed home to bed!

Randy normally attended church services in Lexington at Anchor Baptist Church, which ironically used as it's symbol an anchor cross. Having not gotten home until almost 5 am, he knew he needed to sleep in, and slept until almost noon.

Upon waking, his first thoughts went back to his amazing trace of the Seibert cross apparently made from gold blessed by the Lord. He got dizzy just thinking about it. He wanted to call his good friend Pastor Raymond Bell and tell the origin of the cross to him, but he knew he would still be conducting his church service at New Hope Baptist. So he prepared himself a nice brunch, and enjoyed a bit of leisure and reading the morning papers until around 1:30 pm. He then thought it would be a good time perhaps to catch Raymond.

Raymond answered on the first ring, "Pastor Bell".

"Good afternoon my friend," said Randy. "I've once again got some almost unbelievable information to share with you!"

Raymond responded, "For some reason I feel it might be related to the golden anchor cross."

"Right you are," replied Randy, and he explained in great detail his research and findings from the previous evening.

"Good Lord in heaven," said Pastor Bell. "Am I to understand that the cross that Kylie currently has on a necklace around his neck is likely made from gold cast by Constantine the Great that traces all the way back to St. Peter, and even likely to have been blessed by our Lord?"

"That's it precisely, my friend," replied Randy.

"If I were standing I would now say I needed to sit," said Raymond. "Since I'm sitting, maybe I need to lie down! I'm speechless!"

"I sort of thought you would be Raymond," said Randy. "This is a finding of major importance, and I'm not exactly sure what our next step should be. Any thoughts?"

"What comes to mind is that Sheriff Sterling intends to release pictures of the cross to the media tomorrow and they'll be in the Tuesday papers and on tv. When that happens, your office will be flooded with calls about it. My thought is that you might wish to come to Harlan again on Tuesday. If you're out of the office your secretary would have a good excuse to keep the media off your back until we decide the best course in view of your recent findings. How does that sound?" Raymond asked.

"You read my mind, Raymond," replied Randy. "I'll bring written copies of my findings with me and leave first thing Tuesday morning. I should see you at your church around 11 am. Maybe you should set up a meeting with the sheriff, Is that o.k.?"

"Sounds like a plan to me," said the pastor. "See you Tuesday morning my friend!"

35.

When Carolyn got off work on Monday afternoon she went as always to her mother's house in Wallins to pick up Kylie. She was now worried for his safety. The meeting with Sheriff Sterling had pretty much established that someone had entered Kylie's bedroom last night and used chloroform on Kylie and attempted to steal his anchor cross. That was scary. And to make matters worse, she didn't know any explanation as to how the intruder could have gotten into the house without a key, and Snake was the only other person with a key to their house, although he was suppose to be in Knoxville. When she got to Mawie's she tooted her horn, and Kylie came running out the door and jumped into the car. Her mother appeared at the door and waved. Carolyn waved back and they started home.

"Kylie I'm worried about what happened last night," Carolyn said. "I talked with the sheriff today and we both concluded that someone entered our house and put you to sleep with chloroform and tried to steal your cross. It's still a mystery why they left the cross, but I worry that they might try again. I want to keep you safe, and I know you want to keep the cross. I just don't know what else to do."

Kylie replied, "Don't worry Mom, I can't explain it, but I feel perfectly safe so long as I have my cross. I just know we'll be o.k. Please don't worry ..... that makes me feel bad."

Carolyn reached across the front seat of the car and patted Kylie's knee, and said, "Honey I'm glad you feel that way, and I just hope you're right. But tonight I'd feel a lot better if you would sleep with me. I don't think I would sleep a wink thinking about you upstairs in bed all to yourself. Would you do that for mother?"

Kylie looked a bit sad and thought, and then said, "Well, maybe just for tonight. Would that be o.k.?"

"I think so, honey, thank you," Carolyn replied as she pulled into their driveway. They both got out and went into their house.

Down the road a short distance at Maggard's grocery Fatso sat watching the early news on television. It was just about time to close for the day, it had been a slow one.

Pretty Boy and Trigger came bounding out of the back room headed for the front door.

"You lock up, Fatso. We're calling it a day," Pretty Boy said as they approached the door on their way out.

"I had a tourist stop in a few minutes ago and asked me, 'How do you get to Lexington?'," said Fatso. "I told him I usually got my son to take me." Fatso chuckled.

Pretty Boy and Trigger grunted and went out the door.

It was just before 5 p.m., and as Fatso glanced at the television he saw a picture of a beautiful golden anchor cross. He quickly turned up the volume in time to hear Barbara Clark say, *"These photographs were received just moments ago from Harlan County Sheriff J. Bert Sterling. As he promised at his press conference last Saturday, these are pictures of the extraordinary artifact that was found in the burned remains of the wagon belonging to Harlan County pioneer Reverend Karl Seibert. Reverend Seibert and his wife disappeared in 1798, and their remains were just recently discovered. I have placed a call to the office of Dr. Randy Peters, Director of the Center for Appalachian Research at the University of Kentucky, to try and get additional information about this beautiful historical cross. As soon as I have something new I'll pass it along. Stay tuned ...... this is Barbara Clark for Channel 27 news."*

Fatso turned the television off, and thought, "That thing has got to be worth a fortune. Pretty Boy's missing the boat on this one." He turned everything off, went out the door, locked it, and headed for his car.

Ape reached up and stroked Preacher Puss. "You hold down the fort," he said to the cat as he started out the door.

Bill Black had arrived a few minutes ago for the evening shift in the sheriff's office, and Rosie had departed for the day. Mousy Giles was on patrol. Sheriff Sterling was just coming into the front office when his cell phone rang.

"This is Sheriff Sterling," he said.

"Yes, that would work fine Pastor, I'll plan on arriving at your office tomorrow morning around 11 am. Thanks for setting it up. I'm sure Dr. Peters will have an interesting update for us."

"I'm out of here Bill," said the sheriff. "Keep all the bad guys under control."

"Do my best Bert," Bill replied.

36.

Tuesday morning arrived as a glorious summer day in Harlan. The weather weenies had promised a clear and typically warm day, with a high temperature of about 85 degrees.

Bad Eye shouted to his three sleeping comrades, "Get your lazy asses up. We've got plans to go over. Friday is only three days off .... our retirement is almost here!"

Bad Eye had been up for about an hour already, and had consumed several cups of coffee. He fired up a cigar and watched Snake, Jones, and Billie stir about in their makeshift bunks on the other side of the room. They had been hiding at the junk yard now since Saturday, and were beginning to smell a little rank, since the junk yard offered no shower. But Bad Eye had visions of frolicking in the waters of the warm Caribbean in just a few days, and that helped endure the present stench.

Snake finally got his feet on the floor and stood. Although heavily bandaged, it was obvious he was still strongly favoring his right hand. It hung limply at his side, and Snake had a painful look on his face.

"Hand hurt?" asked Bad Eye.

"Hell no, it feels good," replied Snake sarcastically.

"Well, it better shape up by Friday," Bad Eye said. "You three get yourselves ready for the day and we'll go over the plans again. I've thought of a few details we haven't covered yet. We've got to get this thing down pat."

Snake, Jones, and Billie all grunted and slowly began to move.

Pastor Bell had been up since about 6 am. Betty had already fixed breakfast, and Raymond had gone for a morning jog. He now sat with a cup of coffee at his kitchen table and stared at the front pages of the Lexington Herald-Leader and Knoxville News Sentinel lying in front of him. Both had large pictures of Kylie's golden anchor cross, and stories rehashing finding it in the Seibert ruins. Both stories were accurately reported. Raymond knew there would be similar pictures and a story in today's Harlan Daily Enterprise when it came out later in the day. He thought about how much interest the stories would generate, and his concern for the safety of Kylie and Carolyn came to mind. When he had called Sheriff Sterling late yesterday afternoon to invite him to meet today with Randy, the sheriff had told him about the apparent attempted robbery of the cross the night before at the Potter home. Something else to be concerned about. He finished his coffee, showered, got dressed, gave Betty a hug and kiss, and headed for his office at the church.

At 10:45 Pastor Bell heard the knock on his door.

"Please do come in," he said. "Good morning Randy, I hope the journey over the wilderness trail was pleasant," he said with a smile.

"It was," Randy replied. "And I do still always think about the early pioneers as I journey from Lexington down interstate 75 to Corbin, then highway 25E to Pineville, and finally 119 to Harlan. It's a lot easier today sitting in a comfortable seat going 70 miles per hour with air conditioning .... don't think the pioneers did it that way,"

"But they got to stop and smell the roses," said the pastor.

"True," said Randy, as he took a seat in front of pastor Bell's desk.

"Bert should be along shortly. Before he gets here let me bring you up to date on an attempt to steal Kylie's cross last Sunday night," said Raymond, and he proceeded to relate the story told him by the sheriff.

When Raymond finished, Randy said, "I was concerned that word could leak out about Kylie having the cross, and because it is so valuable worried that something like this might happen. Isn't it interesting that the thief wasn't successful in getting the cross!"

"That is a mystery," said Raymond. "I've given that some thought, and I'll wait till Bert gets here to share those thoughts with you, if that's o.k."

"Sure," said Randy. "Got a soft drink?"

Just as Raymond handed Randy a canned soft drink from the refrigerator in his office, there was another knock on the door, "Anybody home," came the familiar voice of Sheriff Sterling.

"Just us chickens," responded Raymond, as he and Randy stood and shook hands with the sheriff. They all took a seat.

"Raymond was just updating me on the break in at the Potter home last Sunday night," Randy said. "I'm just so pleased that no one was hurt, and that the cross did not get stolen. Raymond was just saying that he had given it some thought and had an idea to share, but wanted to wait until you got here sheriff."

"What do you have in mind, pastor," responded the sheriff.

Raymond started, "You each know the stories about the cross. And I'll go ahead and tell you my thoughts about the unusual things that seem to have occurred to those having possession of the cross, and then Randy has some exciting new information he has uncovered about the origin of the cross. And I can't wait to hear about it."

Pastor Bell leaned back in his chair, paused to gather his thoughts, and then continued, "Let me first quickly review what we know about these unusual events. First off, we know that Karl Seibert said that his father and grandfather told him many stories that involved strange things that occurred to them while wearing the cross, but we have nothing specific. Secondly, Karl Seibert told Samuel Howard about how his fall off a cliff was strangely interrupted and he was delivered without harm to the bottom of the cliff. In this case, Reverend Seibert reported that he felt heat coming from the cross as he held it in his hand after it was blown into his face during his fall. Thirdly, Seibert reported in his letter to Samuel Howard that he had received a vision while wearing the cross wherein he was instructed to make the trip to Mount Pleasant. He specifically said he was holding the cross at the time of the vision and that the cross felt warm. The fourth report was that from Kylie when while he was wearing the cross he attempted to stop his father from hitting his mother with a baseball bat and the bat mysteriously bounced back and knocked out his father. And Kylie said then he felt heat from the cross. And the final report was the one the sheriff just shared about the intruder at the Potter house this past Sunday night. We really don't know what happened, but we do know that Kylie went to bed wearing the cross and that someone came into his bedroom and used chloroform to put Kylie under and apparently then removed the cross, but mysteriously left it behind."

Randy and Bert both nodded their heads in agreement.

Raymond continued, "We also know that the Latin words pax tecum, meaning 'peace be with you', appear on the horizontal arm of the cross. And I remind you that the artifact itself consists of both a cross at the top and an anchor at the bottom. Everyone today associates the cross as being a religious symbol representing the tree upon which Jesus Christ was crucified. Christian believers think that this represents his dying for our sins. The anchor at the bottom was the accepted religious symbol before and after the time of Christ up until about the 4th century AD. So after thinking about the things that occurred to Karl Seibert and apparently to his forefathers, as well as what we know happened to Kylie, the only thing I can conclude is that these strange events are supernatural, and as a Christian believer I think their source was from the Lord. I don't understand the heat associated with each event, but it must have something to do with the dissipation of energy as it passes through the cross. And the Latin words meaning 'peace be with you' seem to agree with each unusual event. In other words, all these events that we know about all seem to relate to good or peaceful outcomes. It's almost like a guardian angel protects the person wearing the cross so long as the outcome furthers peace. Personally, I don't think a crook or evil person wearing the cross would find it of any use in this supernatural way. So maybe that has something to do with why the cross was left by whoever tried to steal it from Kylie last Sunday night. And while this is all speculation on my part, it's the only thing that I can come up with that makes any sense. I would be interested in your thoughts."

The sheriff said, "I had similar thoughts, but not as developed as yours pastor. What you say makes lots of sense to me. But I think it falls into the category of those things that cannot be proven ..... it takes a little faith to understand and believe. What do you think Randy?"

"What I think is that it is time for me to share with you the results of my research on the origin of the cross. My research and what Pastor Bell has just speculated seem to agree exactly."

Randy then passed out copies of the report he generated on the cross's origin. All was quiet for the next several minutes as the sheriff and Raymond read Randy's report.

As he finished reading, Pastor Bell's face seemed to lose color. He looked up from the report and said, "So do I understand that it is likely that the gold in the cross that Kylie has was
actually blessed by Christ and then was presented to St. Peter as he began the church?"

"Exactly," said Randy.

"I think I may faint," said Pastor Bell.

"I'll catch you," the sheriff said. Then he added, "Randy, this is an excellent piece of detective work! It looks like you've accurately traced the Seibert golden anchor cross as being cast by Constantine the Great using gold given to him by Pope Sylvester I, which in turn had been passed through the Catholic church all the way back to St. Peter, and that St. Peter had been given the gold after it received the Lord's blessing to help start the church. How astounding!"

Randy gave a big smile and said, "Everything just seems to fit. Certainly Raymond's belief that the strange events are likely supernatural in origin, and that the gold from the cross was actually blessed by our Lord would seem to go hand in hand, so to speak." Raymond and Bert both nodded approval.

Bert then spoke, "It would be my advice, based upon Randy's report and Raymond's interpretation, that we make public the information in Randy's report. I think our explanation about the supernatural events associated with the cross should remain with us, since it requires religious belief, and many of the public would simply reject it as unfounded."

"I agree," said Randy. "As we discussed previously, my report will eventually be made public anyway, since I work for a state supported institution. But there is no need to release any information about the events associated with the cross. These may surface in time, but they don't need to be released now."

"I will agree with all you say," said Raymond. "I'm still trying to absorb all this. From my religious perspective this is simply beyond magnificent."

Bert then said, "Yeah, we all need to think about all this more, but my feeling is that it would be good and proper to go ahead now and release Randy's research findings on the cross's origin. After the photographs that were in the papers and on television today, the public will be clamoring for more information, and Randy's report has all the answers. Do you two agree?"

"Yes," they said in unison.

And then Raymond added, "The only down side to all this fantastic information is that it just makes Kylie's cross more and more valuable, and I get seriously concerned for his safety, and for that of his mother. Who ever tried to steal the cross Sunday night is still out there, and now there will be many more trying to identify the owner of the cross."

"Ditto those remarks," said the sheriff. "I'll call Carolyn and tell her about everything we've discussed today, and tell her to be extra careful. With luck all this will blow over before too long."

All three men stood, shook hands, said parting remarks, and went their separate ways. Randy traveled back to Lexington, the sheriff went to his office and sent out another press release with Randy's report attached, and Pastor Bell sat in his office and pondered the astounding events that had occurred.

37.

Sheriff Sterling had gotten to the office early on Wednesday morning, arriving around 7 am. Rosie and Ape had not arrived yet, but as Bert entered the door Preacher Puss served as the welcoming committee, giving forth with meow after meow and rubbing gently at Bert's ankle. Bert had come to love the cat, and he reached down and picked her up and stroked her gently as she cranked up her motor. The sheriff then reached down on Rosie's desk and picked up a package of Whisker Lickins that Rosie kept as treats for Preacher Puss and extracted several and placed them on the floor. She woofed them down quickly. Bert then picked her up and placed her on her shelf located between the door and window. He then reached down and picked up copies of the Lexington and Knoxville papers that had been placed through the slot in the front door. The Harlan paper would not arrive until afternoon. Bert made coffee, and after turning on the coffee maker he went into his office with the newspapers. He was anxious to see the stories about the golden anchor cross origin based upon Dr. Peters' report that he had faxed to them yesterday afternoon. He had watched Barbara Clark's report on the Lexington television station last night .... and it was sensational. She had gotten two professors, one from

Asbury Theological Seminary in Wilmore, Kentucky and the other from the Lexington Theological Seminary in Lexington to discuss the report from Dr. Peters. Both professors were astounded at the revelation of finding a golden anchor cross in Harlan, Kentucky that could be traced back to receiving a blessing from Christ. The segment took almost the entire time allotted for the news last evening, and the final statements by the professors seemed to support Randy's conclusions, but they did say they would like very much to be able to physically examine the cross, and were also very curious as to its present whereabouts. Ms. Clark assured them and the television audience that she would be looking into that.

Both newspapers had front page coverage of the golden anchor cross origin. The headlines read,

Cross found in Harlan traced back to a
blessing by Christ, in the _Lexington Herald-Leader_, and
Harlan Golden Cross Traced Back to Jesus, in the
Knoxville News-Sentinel.

Both newspapers printed verbatim Dr. Peter's report that Bert had faxed to them, and then they added their own commentary, with each including statements offered by religious historians in their cities. The net result was that each article appeared very positive and well written. Bert was pleased with the media stories.

Rosie stuck her head in Bert's office and said, "Well, aren't you the early bird today."

"Early bird gets the worm," replied the sheriff. "Don't give Preacher Puss any more Whisker Lickins, I already fed him a handful. That cat's getting fat!"

"I'd like to look at those newspapers when you're finished," Rosie said.

"Take em," the sheriff replied. "I've read what I was interested in," and handed Rosie both papers.

"I can guess what that was," she said as she took the papers back to her desk.

Ape came into the sheriff's office and said, "Bert, I read the morning papers earlier at home, and I think we can expect hordes of folks coming into the county looking for gold. Most will likely wind up around Wallins. You think maybe me and Simpson should head that way to make sure things don't get out of hand?"

"Yeah, that's probably a good idea Ape. If we need you for anything I'll give you a call. Just drive around the Wallins area so that people will be reinforced that we're there," Bert said.

"I'll call Simpson and tell him to head over here and pick me up and we'll be gone," Ape replied. "See you a little later."

"Take care," Bert responded.

Deputies Cornett and Brown were driving toward Wallins on highway 119. They were just a few miles from Wallins when Simpson Brown said, "Ape, Maggard's Grocery is just ahead. How about pulling in there a minute and let's get something to drink and maybe a donut."

"O.K. by me," Ape replied, and a minute later pulled into the front of Maggard's Grocery. The two deputies then walked in.

Fatso said, "Well, well ..... if it ain't Harlan County's finest. What brings you boys to our establishment today?"

"Just wanted something to drink and maybe a donut, Fatso. That o.k. with you?" Ape responded.
"Just help yourself, boys," said Fatso. "By the way, you know what has two grey legs and two brown legs?"

Ape and Simpson starred at Fatso. "An elephant with diarrhea," Fatso said as he burst out laughing.

"Ha, ha, ha," said Simpson. Ape grunted. Fatso continued to laugh.

The deputies got their refreshments, and brought them to the counter to pay Fatso. When they placed the drinks and donuts on the counter Fatso asked, "You boys in the neighborhood because of that nice golden cross Kylie Potter found?"

"We're here to make sure all stays peaceful, Fatso. What makes you think Kylie Potter found the cross?" asked Ape.

"Little birdie told me," said Fatso.

"Little birdie might be wrong," said Ape as he and Simpson paid for their purchases.

"Could be, but I don't think so," said Fatso as he gave them their change. "You want a bag?"

"No need," said Simpson, and he and Ape walked out and got back in the cruiser.

"I can't believe that Fatso Chapel knows Kylie has the cross," said Ape. Both he and Simpson had been briefed and were aware that Kylie did, in fact, have it. "I'd better call Bert and tell him." Ape pulled the microphone and called the sheriff.

"Bert, we just stopped here at Maggard's Grocery, and ole Fatso asked us if we were here looking around because of the cross that Kylie Potter found," reported Ape.

"Thanks for letting me know, Ape," Bert answered. "We knew that Carolyn's mother, Mawie, had accidently told Fatso. He probably blabs it to all his customers. Too bad. Keep me posted on anything else you find out."

"Will do," Ape replied and signed off. The deputies drove toward Wallins.

At about 4 pm Ape and Simpson were sitting in the cruiser parked at the corner of Puckett Avenue and state highway 219 in Wallins. They had a good view of Carolyn's mom's house, located not far from the intersection of the two streets.

Ape picked up the microphone and called the sheriff, "Hey Bert, Simpson and I are sitting here in Wallins watching the circus. There are people everywhere. There are so many cars there are no more parking places, and cars are just cruising around. Most of the license plates are from out of the county, and many from Tennessee. People are walking up and down the streets looking for locals to talk with about the Seibert ruins."

Bert replied, "I hope the crowd is at least orderly, and can you see Mawie's house from where you're parked?"

Ape said, "Yeah, everyone's behaving as far as I can tell. And yes, we have a clear view of Mawies house. One couple went up to her door and knocked, and she came to the door and talked to them for a bit. I was curious and walked over as the couple left and asked them what business they had at her house. The man responded that they had stopped by Maggard's Grocery before getting here, and apparently Fatso blabbed all about Kylie having found the cross and that he frequently stayed with his grandmother and told them where she lived. They were asking if they could see the cross. Mawie told them he was not here. I guess that was a bit of a fib, since this is a workday and when Carolyn is at work Kylie is usually here. But we haven't seen him."

"I do think he is there," Bert replied. "Please keep a close watch, that cross is extremely valuable and I sure don't want anything happening to Kylie or Mawie."

Ape replied, "Will do. And you might want to send Mousy Giles over here to relieve us when he starts his shift. These lookies will likely be around at least until dark. Or do you want me and Simpson to work overtime?"

Bert said, "I hate to ask, but I feel we may need more manpower at least until dark. If you two don't mind, I'd like for you to hang out there until around dark and then give me a call. I'll use Mousy to patrol around the area, especially around the Potter house. I'm worried about Carolyn picking up Kylie after work and then going home."

"Simpson said it was fine with him to do overtime, and it suits me as well," Ape replied. "And don't worry, we'll keep an eye on Mawie's house and when Carolyn gets here we'll escort Kylie to her car and see that they get off without incident."

"You guys are the best," said the sheriff as he ended the call.

The sheriff sat back in his chair and thought about the situation. He then picked up his phone and called Carolyn. He had her cell phone number. She answered and said she was just getting off work, and he told her about all the tourists hanging out in Wallins, and alerted her that she should be careful when she picked up Kylie, but that Ape and Simpson were there and would escort him to her car. She seemed grateful, but the sheriff detected great worry in her voice as well.

The sheriff had a television in his office and he usually kept it tuned to either the Lexington station or to Fox News. Currently it was the latter, and as the news came on the lead story was the Seibert golden anchor cross. A picture of it filled the screen as the announcer traced it from its biblical origin to Harlan County. Bert thought, "Oh boy, now it's gone national. Things are likely to really start popping now!"

Bert turned the television off, grabbed his hat, and headed for the front door.

Bill Black had replaced Rosie in the front office for the evening shift. As the sheriff passed through he said, "Bill I'm headed toward Wallins, give me a call if you need me."

Bill responded that he would.

The sheriff drove to Maggard's Grocery. He entered just before 5 pm. Fatso was just starting to close up shop.

"Afternoon Sheriff," Fatso said as he closed the cash register. "Just ready to call it a day."

Bert replied, "Fatso, I know that Carolyn Potter's mother had a conversation with you, and that she indicated Kylie Potter was the person that found the golden anchor cross. And I know that you have told several people about it, including strangers that have stopped here at the store. This could result in causing big problems for Carolyn, her mother, and certainly for Kylie. I'm going to ask you to please stop talking to anyone about the story. I know you don't have to honor my request, but in the interest of safety for the kid and his family I'd sure appreciate your keeping quiet."

"Sheriff, I didn't know I was causing any problem..... just hadn't thought about it like that," Fatso said. "And you can count on me .... I'll button my lip. Mum's the word."
"Thanks, Fatso, that will be a big help," Bert replied.

"Hey Sheriff," Fatso said. "Know what time it is when an elephant sits on your watch?"

"Time to get a new watch!" Bert replied.

Fatso giggled, and said, "You a smart man sheriff"

The sheriff left and Fatso closed up Maggard's Grocery for the day.

38.

At about 5:15 pm Bert arrived at Mawie's house. Just a few minutes later Carolyn showed up to gather Kylie. Bert got out of his cruiser, waved to Ape and Simpson parked across the road, and walked to Mawie's door to accompany Kylie. Several people milling around on the street gathered outside Mawie's fence to watch as the sheriff and Kylie strolled off the porch down the walk and out to Carolyn's car.

"Special delivery," said the sheriff, as Kylie popped in his mother's car.

"Many thanks," Carolyn replied with a worried look on her face.

"I'll follow you home, and make sure you get inside there all safely," Bert said.

"I do greatly appreciate it," Carolyn replied, and started her car moving. Bert got in his cruiser and followed closely behind them.

When they got to the Potter house there were about a dozen people standing outside around the house. Bert got out of his cruiser and shouted to the crowd to please disperse. About half turned and appeared to be leaving, the other half just stood where they were. Carolyn and Kylie had remained seated in her car in the driveway. Bert went to their car and opened Carolyn's door and told them to get out. The three walked into the house.

"I feel sure those folks out there are just curious, Carolyn, but I think I'll stay here with you for a while if you don't mind," Bert said.

"No, I certainly don't mind. I feel totally safe with you here Bert," she said. "How about having dinner with us?"

"Best offer I've had today," the sheriff responded. The three then relaxed, and Carolyn started preparing dinner.

The crowds continued to escalate in Wallins. As dusk began to set in, Ape called Bert and told him there was still a lot of people milling around in Wallins, but that the crowd remained orderly. The sheriff asked Ape if he and Simpson would be willing to stay on until 10 pm, and they agreed. Bert told them he was at the Potter house with Carolyn and Kylie, and would be leaving there shortly.

The rest of Wednesday evening remained quiet, although there appeared to be lots of strangers still hanging around.

Thursday morning the sheriff was in his office early. Ape and Rosie reported for duty at about a quarter of eight. Rosie stuck her head in the sheriff's office and said, "I watched both the local and cable television news programs last night, and they all carried breaking news stories about the cross, it's origin, and lots of stuff about Harlan County and it's history. We're getting famous!"

"Publicity I could do without," said the sheriff as he sipped a cup of coffee.

Ape came in and sat in front of the sheriff's desk and said, "Bert, today's going to be worse than yesterday. We might have to close down Wallins .... I don't think we will be able to handle all the traffic. What'd you think?"

"I think you and Simpson should go back there and see how things look. If traffic really starts to back up all the way to 119 then go ahead and put up a road block and only let locals in. And keep me posted," said the sheriff.

"I'm on it," Ape said as he pulled his phone to call Simpson to pick him up.

Bert then placed a call to Carolyn, and she answered on the first ring.

"Just checking in Carolyn, did you two have a good evening?" asked Bert.

"Everything was quiet, but I had a terrible time sleeping," she said. "Probably only slept a couple of hours. I think Kylie slept o.k. The two of us are headed for the bank now. I decided that I wouldn't chance leaving him with mother today and called Calvin Brown at his home this morning and asked if it would be o.k. if Kylie came to work with me. He said it would be fine, and said Kylie could stay in our conference room. There's a television in there, and I brought him some books and games as well. I'll feel a lot better knowing he's safe. I also asked Calvin if he could come tomorrow as well, and he said no problem. Hopefully by next Monday maybe things will have calmed down and we can get back to normal. What do you think?"

"You are a very smart lady," Bert said. "I don't know now if things will be better by Monday, but we can keep our fingers crossed. Just call me if you need anything."

"Thanks Bert, you're an angel," she replied, and they continued their drive to Harlan.

"Boys, I can smell all that money!" said Bad Eye. "We've gone over and over our plans for tomorrow, and I feel good about it."

"Can't be soon enough," said Snake. "I need to get to the Bahamas to get some r&r, and get my hand healed."

"Won't be as long as it has been," said Jones. "You going to be o.k. with that hand tomorrow?"

"That's a fool thing to ask," said Snake. "It is what it is, and I'll get by just fine. It just still hurts like hell"

"Hope it's not infected," Billie commented.

Snake nodded and said nothing. Bad Eye said, "Well, we should be loading everything up so we'll be all set for tomorrow. I think we should sleep in tomorrow morning, then get up and have a big brunch, then just lay around and take it easy until about 3:45. We leave here then we'll be in town by 4:15 easy, and we can get parked and wait to make our move at 4:25, all agreed?"

Snake, Jones, and Billy nodded.

By 2 pm on Thursday afternoon Ape and Simpson decided Wallins could not take any more traffic. They had called Bert and told him the situation, and his instructions were for Simpson to sit on Mawie's porch and not let anyone inside her yard, and for Ape to drive to the intersection of 219 and 119 and place the cruiser across the entrance to 219 and only let locals enter. The sheriff had called Mousy Giles on duty, and had sent him to stand guard outside the Potter residence. The circus had begun in earnest. Television crews had arrived from stations in Huntington, West Virginia, Knoxville, Tennessee, and Lexington and Louisville Kentucky. Their satellite antenna trucks were parked all over Wallins. Reporters with cameramen trailing were going from house to house trying to get locals to give interviews. Mawie stayed in her house, letting Simpson keep anyone off her property. Sheriff Sterling kept close tabs on all his deputies by calling each one about every 30 minutes to check their situations. Although hordes of people had descended on Wallins, all seemed to be orderly, and for that the sheriff was indeed thankful.

The sheriff parked his cruiser outside Miners Bank at 4:30 and waited for Carolyn and Kylie to come out. As soon as he saw them leaving he stepped from his car and said, "Your escort at your service! I'll follow you two home, just to be on the safe side. Mousy is standing by outside your house, so you'll be safe once you get home. I'll be back at your house in the morning around 7:30 to escort you back to the bank, and will give you another escort home tomorrow afternoon. By Monday hopefully things will have settled down and we can all get back to our normal routines. Drive carefully, I'll be right behind you."

Carolyn thanked Bert, and then she and Kylie walked to her car, parked only a short distance down the street, got in and pulled out for home. Bert followed them.

39.

Friday morning things seemed well under control. By dark last night most of the visitors had left. The sheriff kept Mousy at the Potter residence and Simpson at Mawie's house until about 11 pm, and then told them to call it a day. This morning he had escorted Carolyn and Kylie back to Miner's Bank, and had sent Ape and Simpson back to Wallins to keep watch on activity there. The sheriff then went back to his office.

"Wow," Rosie said as the sheriff walked into the office. "Hard to believe how much publicity our little town is getting. It's exciting to see all the strangers and to watch the stories on television. You doing o.k. Bert?"

"Yeah, but I'll be doing better when everything gets back to normal," the sheriff replied. "Don't know when that'll be, of course."

Preacher Puss meowed loudly as she rubbed against the sheriff's ankle. He reached down and rewarded her with a pet.

"Bet Ape and Simpson are getting tired of Wallins," Rosie said.

Bert replied, "I suppose, but they've done a great job keeping the peace there ..... and they've sure put in the overtime, and with no complaints. They're good eggs."

Bert walked in his office and took a seat behind his desk. He had grabbed a cup of coffee on the way in. As soon as he sat down his cell phone rang. It was Pastor Bell just checking in, and Bert gave him an update on everything.

"If we can just get through today, then hopefully over the weekend things will die down," Bert spoke to Pastor Bell.

"O.K., thanks for calling. I'll keep you posted on anything new," the sheriff said to Raymond and then clicked off his cell phone.

At 3:30 Friday afternoon Bad Eye and the boys had Billie's car all loaded. Billie had a 10 year old SUV. Billie was a good mechanic, and kept the vehicle in good shape, and it had lots of room for their suitcases.

Bad Eye said, "Boys, that's it. We're good to go. We do a little business at the bank, drive to Knoxville, and away to the Bahamas. How sweet it will be!"

Billie, Jones, and Snake all got big grins on their faces. Bad Eye had locked up everything at the junk yard, and they got in Billie's car and started down the driveway to the gate. At the gate Bad Eye got out, opened the gate after looking to see that no one was around, and then closed the gate back after Billie pulled his car through it. Bad Eye got in the passenger's seat, Snake and Jones were sitting in the back seat, and Billie pulled out onto 119 headed for Harlan.

Because they were running a few minutes ahead of schedule, Billie pulled over to the side of the road and parked to let about 10 minutes pass. They then started again for the bank, right on schedule. At about 4:20 Billie was able to find a parking place just a couple of spaces down from the entrance to the bank. At exactly 4:25 Jones got out of the back seat and walked to the bank, entered, and walked over to a table to start making out his fake deposit slip. He pulled the stack of checks that Bad Eye had given him, and started to write each one down on the deposit ticket. He looked around in the lobby, and was pleased to see only one elderly lady talking with Julie Lacey as she was concluding her business. Gut Blankenship, the guard, was sitting on a stool close to the front door. Jones could see that Calvin Brown was in his office, and Carolyn Potter was at her teller station. Then he heard what sounded like a television, and glanced at the conference room and saw Kylie sitting in a chair watching television. "Well, there's one thing we didn't count on," he thought. But I think we can handle a kid. Jones slowly pulled his derringer out and placed it under the deposit slip. He wasn't worried about Gut seeing it, since he was pretty much both blind and deaf.

Calvin Brown stood up from his desk and walked into the lobby following the elderly lady over to the door.

"That time, Gut," Calvin said.

"Huh," said Gut.

Calvin raised his voice to the point of shouting and repeated, "Time to close, Gut".

Gut nodded and continued to sit on his stool.

Calvin then turned the door sign over such that the word CLOSED appeared on the outside. He then walked back to his office.

Jones gathered his checks and deposit slip and held them in his left hand while holding the derringer in his right hand under the deposit slip, and began walking toward the front door and Gut. When he reached the door he dropped the checks and deposit slip, opened the door with his left hand, and stuck the derringer to the side of Gut's head and shouted, "First person that does anything causes Gut to get shot."

As Bad Eye, Snake, and Billie walked in the door they put on their ski masks. Billie ran to Calvin Brown's office and held a pistol in his face. Julie and Carolyn both looked stunned, but neither screamed or moved. Bad Eye quickly moved behind the tellers and started to tie their hands behind their backs. Snake tried to help Bad Eye, but he had to put his gun back in his belt and assist with his good hand, his right hand still heavily bandaged. Jones tied up Gut, put a piece of cloth in his mouth and then unrolled duct tape over his mouth and around his head, and then pushed him down on the floor after taking his gun and sticking it in his belt. Billie had tied up Calvin Brown. Bad Eye and Snake were putting blindfolds on the tellers when they heard a voice, "Mommy, are they hurting you?"

Snake recognized the voice immediately, and turned to see Kylie standing at the door of the conference room. Snake grabbed his gun from his belt and pointed it at Kylie and said, "Lay on the floor, boy."

Kylie recognized Snake's voice and said, "Dad, is that you?" As he dropped to the floor.

Jones then walked over to Kylie and put duct tape around his hands, mouth, and eyes.

Billie stuck the barrel of his gun on Calvin Brown's forehead and said, "You know what this is on your forehead?"

"I think it's called a gun," Calvin said.

Billie said, "Do as I ask and no one will be hurt. I want the pass key to the safe deposit boxes. I know you have it, and if you don't produce it right now we'll start killing your employees one at a time, starting with Gut Blankenship. You understand?"

"That won't be necessary," Calvin said. "The pass key is in the bottom left drawer of my desk. It's the one with the red ribbon on it."

Billie then told Jones to wrap duct tape around Calvin's mouth and eyes and sit him in his chair. Billie then reached down and opened the bottom left desk drawer. He saw the key immediately, with a strip of red ribbon tied to it.

"Got it'" shouted Billie, as he and Jones walked toward the vault.

The four entered the vault, and using the pass key started opening safe deposit boxes. Normally the boxes required two keys, one from the bank and one from the box owner, but the special pass key was a long, cylindrical steel key that entered into a round hole at the top right side of each box. When it was inserted the box could be removed.

Bad Eye had opened the box of trash bags and handed one to Billie and Jones and opened one for himself. Snake, using his good left hand, went through the safe deposit boxes inserting the pass key and then pulling the boxes out. The other three came along behind and dumped the box contents into their bags. When they came to the two large boxes owned by Pretty Boy their eyes bulged as they opened them and saw package after package of 100 dollar bills. They shouted with glee, and hurriedly finished up emptying all the boxes. Many only contained papers, and these were simply dumped on the floor. Some had jewelry, which was dumped in the trash bags along with the cash. Most had at least some cash.

When they finished in the vault they headed for the cashier's windows and pulled all the cash from their drawers. They then tied a knot in all the trash bags.

"O.K.," said Bad Eye. "We've done it, now let's get everyone in the vault and get out of here."

Billie walked in to get Calvin Brown, Bad Eye picked up each of the tellers, and Jones walked over and pulled up Kylie. All were herded into the vault. Snake reached with his good left hand to pull Gut up off the floor, but soon realized he couldn't do it.

"Someone give me a hand here," Snake said. "Ole Gut weights a ton, I can't budge him."

"Just leave him," said Bad Eye. "He can't see or hear, so he don't know anything. Just leave him there in the floor."

So all four walked to the entrance to the vault. Calvin Brown, Julie Lacey, and Carolyn and Kylie Potter were all standing in the vault with their hands tied behind their backs and their mouths and eyes covered with duct tape.

Snake secretly looked at the bulge in Kylie's shirt and wished he could relieve him of the golden cross, but feeling the hurt in his right hand he thought he better leave well enough alone.

"O.K., lets close the vault and get the heck out of dodge," said Bad Eye as he reached for the vault door. He closed the door. And then he started to turn the wheel to lock it.

Sheriff Sterling pulled up outside the bank at 4:35 pm. He was five minutes late to escort Carolyn and Kylie home, but had failed to call Carolyn to tell her he was running a bit late. He saw her car still parked down the street, so he just sat in his cruiser waiting for the two of them to come out. At 4:50 he began to get a bit worried, and pulled out his cell phone and tried to call her. No answer. It was a beautiful, warm, clear summer afternoon, but just as Bert was getting out of his cruiser to go to the bank there was a tremendous bolt of lightning that struck the bank building with a roar so loud it pushed the sheriff back against his car. He regained his position and started running to the bank. He pushed the door open and entered the lobby. There to his left on the floor sat Gut Blankenship with a puzzled look on his face. Bert walked quickly behind the teller's counter and saw three hooded figures and one without a hood lying on the floor. Beside them there were three very large trash bags that looked to be full of something. The four on the floor were not moving. Bert rolled them over and pulled their masks off. He recognized all except the one without the mask. He then grabbed the large roll of duct tape laying on the tellers counter and began taping their hands behind their backs. Each of them seemed to have a pulse ..... apparently just knocked out. He then walked back around to Gut Blankenship.

Bert reached down and untied Gut's hands, and then pulled the tape off his mouth. Gut spit the cloth out of his mouth, and started breathing hard. Bert then pulled as hard as he could on Gut's arms to get him upright. Finally Gut was standing.

"Boy, was that something!" Gut said.

"What happened, Gut?" asked the sheriff.

"Well, those men in the floor over there came in here and robbed the bank. Calvin, Julie, Carolyn, and her son are in the vault," Gut said as he pointed toward the vault.

The sheriff turned and ran to the vault, grabbed the large wheel, and pulled on the door. It opened. To his amazement, there stood four people with duct tape over their eyes and mouths, and with their hands tied behind their backs. He quickly released each of them. He then took out his cell phone and called Rosie, requesting assistance from the Harlan City Police and the Kentucky State Police.

The City and State Police arrived within ten minutes. The junk yard gang was turned over to the Kentucky State Police charged with attempted bank robbery. All four bank employees and Kylie sat in chairs in the bank's conference room. Bert was with them.

The sheriff said, "I know you each need rest, and I'll let you go shortly. I just need to ask a few questions first, if you'll permit me."

All nodded affirmatively.

The sheriff continued, "I think it's obvious that Bad Eye Cawood and his buddies tried to rob the bank, and I'll get details about all of this later, after you've recovered. But could you just give me an initial statement as to what happened?"

Gut Blankenship spoke up, "Sheriff, I might be in the best position right now to tell you what happened. Most people think I'm blind and deaf, but that's not exactly true. A few months back I got cataract surgery in both eyes and got the latest in hearing aids for both ears, so I can now see and hear pretty well. Course I now need to find a diet that works, but that's another story. Anyway, I was sitting on my stool and Calvin Brown came over to put the CLOSED sign in the door. He spoke to me and out of habit I said 'huh', but I heard him. The next thing I know this one fellow sticks a gun to my head and threatens everyone in the bank that he'll shoot me if they don't cooperate. They tie up everyone, then get the pass key from Calvin for the safe deposit boxes, then loot everything into those garbage bags, then put everyone except me in the vault. They thought I didn't see or hear them, and that I was too fat to get up off the floor. Well, they was right about me being too fat to get up off the floor with my hands tied behind me, but they was wrong thinking I couldn't hear or see. I was watching them as they closed the vault door. They were just getting ready to turn the wheel to lock the door when the damnest thing happened. It was like each of the four just got plugged into an electrical outlet. I saw streaks of what looked just like bolts of lightning flash into each of them. Then they just all slumped to the floor. Out like a lamp. Beats all I ever did see."

"Gut, that's all I need to hear right now," Bert said. "Thank you very much. Now I want each of you to go home and get some rest .... you've had a very hard day. I'm just so glad that none of you were hurt. And we did catch the bad guys, and even recovered all the money. We'll have plenty of time to talk about everything later. I'll be in touch."

Bert walked all out of the bank, and helped Carolyn and Kylie into their car. Carolyn said, "Bert, I just can't believe Snake was involved in that, and that he was prepared to take the lives of his wife and son."

Bert replied, "Sad, sad. There is evil in this world, and we've surely seen our share of it today. You two get home and get rested. I'm just so glad you weren't hurt. And Kylie still has his cross!"

Kylie looked at the sheriff and said, "And it's still warm!"

40.

It was Saturday at 3 pm. The combination of the attempted bank robbery and the interest in the golden anchor cross had caused Sheriff Sterling to call a press conference. The interest was so great that the sheriff asked the Harlan High School superintendent for permission to use their gymnasium. Permission was granted, and a large long table was set up at one end of the gym with chairs to accommodate Sheriff Sterling, Pastor Raymond Bell, Dr. Randy Peters, Carolyn and Kylie Potter, and Calvin Brown. The six now sat at the table facing a bank of cameras, microphones, photographers, and numerous reporters. The lights facing the six were blinding.

Sheriff Sterling took the portable microphone and started the press conference, "I want to thank each of you for taking the time to be here today. As I know you are well aware, we have had some interesting things going on in our little community over the past few days." Chuckles were heard from the crowd. "I thought the best way to discuss these and to answer your questions would be to have this press conference today. I think we will be able to provide you the answers you seek."

Bert continued, "Please let me first introduce to you those here with me today. The gentleman seated beside me is Mr. Calvin Brown. Mr. Brown is president of the Harlan Miners Bank. Next to him is Pastor Raymond Bell of Harlan's New Hope Baptist Church. Next is Dr. Randy Peters, Director of the University of Kentucky's Center for Appalachian Research. The lady sitting next to Randy is Mrs. Carolyn Potter, and finally, but certainly not least, other than in stature, is her son Kylie Potter. To start with, I think we should start with yesterday's attempted bank robbery. I'll ask Mr. Brown if he will address that."

Calvin Brown said, "Thanks Bert. At closing time, just about 4:30 yesterday afternoon, four men entered our bank and attempted to rob it. They were successful in their plan in that they were able to gather all the money both in the bank and in our safe deposit boxes. They then placed myself and two bank tellers, including Mrs. Potter here, and her son Kylie, who was visiting at the bank, into the vault. We were tied up and blindfolded. Our security guard, Mr. Gut Blankenship, was tied up, gagged, and left sitting on the floor of the lobby. They then closed the vault door, but before they could lock it there apparently was some type of electrical malfunction which, fortunately for us, resulted in shocking all four of the robbers. The shock was sufficient to completely knock them out. Sheriff Sterling came into the bank at this time. He had been waiting outside to escort Mrs.

Potter and her son home after she got off work. The sheriff saw an electrical discharge and heard a loud noise from the bank, and these caused him to rush into the bank. When he did he was able to tie up and arrest the robbers before they regained consciousness. All of the money they had taken was secured by the sheriff. Sheriff Sterling called the Harlan City Police and the Kentucky State Police and they responded quickly, taking the robbers to jail. Thankfully, no one was injured."

"Thank you Calvin," said the sheriff. "We'll hold questions until all have made a statement. Next I call on Dr. Randy Peters."

The microphone was passed to Randy. "I think each of you has received a copy of the report I made addressing the history of the beautiful golden anchor cross that was found near Wallins in the 1798 ruins that were determined to be those of Reverend Karl Seibert, his wife Mary, and their wagon and possessions. I'm here to answer any questions you might have about that report."

Randy passed the microphone back to the sheriff, who said, "Thanks Randy, next we have Pastor Raymond Bell."

"Because the person that found the golden anchor cross brought it to me seeking advice, I recommended contacting Dr. Peters, knowing him as a friend and an expert on the history of Harlan County. I too will be happy to answer any questions."

Raymond Bell then passed the microphone to Carolyn Potter. "I am the mother of the person that found the golden anchor cross. My son Kylie and I first wished to remain anonymous, but after the events of the past few days have decided, upon consultation with our pastor Raymond Bell, to announce our involvement. We will both be happy also to answer your questions .... but I might have to help Kylie a bit." Carolyn smiled at Kylie, who looked at his mother and forced a smile.

Carolyn passed the microphone to Kylie and said, "Would you like to say anything?"

Kylie slowly reached down the neck of his shirt and gently pulled out the golden anchor cross. The clicks of the camera shutters was almost deafening. Kylie held the cross out in front of him, and the cameras rolled and reporters shuffled around positioning themselves to get better looks.

Kylie then said, "I found this in the woods near Wallins. I've worn it ever since I found it. It's really hard for me to explain, but I just feel so good and safe when I wear it."

The microphone was then passed back to Pastor Raymond Bell, who said, "Thank you Kylie, that was very brave of you. I have talked with Kylie and his mother at length about this beautiful cross. You know it's astounding history. It's value is not the monetary worth of the gold it's made from, although that is substantial. But rather, it's value is derived from the fact that it can be traced back to the time of our Lord, Jesus Christ. And as Randy stated in his report, the gold from which it was cast by Constantine the Great, has been established as having been blessed by our Lord before being passed to St. Peter to help establish the church. The word 'priceless' comes to mind. And I must tell you that it is known that there have been many instances where unexplained events have befallen the wearer of this cross, the last of which was yesterday at the bank when the robbers were rendered unconscious under unusual circumstances just as they attempted to kill 4 people, including Kylie wearing the cross, by sealing them in the bank vault. Being the Christian believers that we are, I join Carolyn and Kylie in thinking these events are somehow directed from above. The beautiful cross bears the Latin words pax tecum, which means 'peace be with you'. Our Lord is the Prince of Peace, and all of the unusual events that are known to have occurred to those wearing this cross are events that support bringing about peaceful outcomes. These events certainly cannot be scientifically explained. They require Christian belief and faith. Carolyn, Kylie, and I have these, and they are sufficient for us. I know there will be those that will disagree. I respect that.

Pastor Bell paused a moment, and then continued, "Because of the priceless value of the cross, I have an important announcement to make. Kylie has asked me to announce that he is giving the cross to the Center for Appalachian Research. Kylie is aware that the cross is too valuable for him to wear, and that keeping it could also place both he and his mother in constant danger from potential thieves. Kylie talked first with his mother about this, and the two of them first wanted to give it to New Hope Baptist Church. When they told me this I was greatly humbled, but explained to them that to put such a treasure on display in a church could be interpreted as worshiping the object, rather than what it represented, and we did not want that. I talked with Dr. Peters about this, and he agreed that it's historical significance could justify its presence in his center. The cross will remain the property of Kylie, but will be placed for permanent viewing and study in a special room to be constructed using monies that were found during the attempted robbery yesterday. I think the sheriff wants to discuss this."

The microphone was again passed to Sheriff Sterling. "After the attempted robbery yesterday, bundles of one hundred dollar bills amounting to about 3.5 million dollars were found that were traced to lock boxes rented by a person that will remain nameless, but when contacted refused to take ownership, saying that the money was planted and did not belong to him. Accordingly, the monies will be divided as follows. 1 million dollars will be given to the Center for Appalachian Research earmarked for construction of a room with displays for the golden anchor cross found by Kylie Potter. 1.5 million dollars will be placed in a trust fund for Kylie Potter with his mother Carolyn as the trustee. The monies in this trust will be used for Kylie's college education, with the remaining balance given to him upon his 25th birthday. The remaining 1 million dollars will go to Harlan County and will be designated for construction of a monument that will address the history of the anchor cross, focusing on its Harlan County connection.

There was silence in the gymnasium. Then there was applause. And then the questions started.

Ten days had passed since the sheriff's press conference. It was now Tuesday, and Bert and Ape were on coffee break at Creech Cafe.

Fred strolled over to the table where the sheriff and his deputy sat, and refilled their coffee cups.

Ape said, "Fred, it's good to see Polly back on the job and looking healthy. Did she get a clean bill of health from the vet?"

"Sure did," said Fred, "and she's back to mooching anything she can from my customers."

"Polly want a cracker, Polly want a cracker, Polly want a cracker," came the reply from Polly perched on her stand by the door.

"Nothing doing Polly," said Ape, "you're getting too fat."

"Polly sad, Polly sad, " the bird replied.

Fred took a seat with Bert and Ape, and said, "It's good to see that things have settled down here in the metropolis. Things sure were popping at the end of last month."

"Couldn't have taken much more, Fred," Bert replied. "We were really stretched thin, and had to call on the City and State Police for help. Yeah, things have settled quite a bit, and I'm extremely thankful."

Fred asked, "I guess the junk yard gang will be spending a good stretch in the big house?"

Bert answered, "Don't think we'll likely see any of them for some time to come. They were all bad eggs, but I did feel sorry for Carolyn having to see Snake involved in that whole thing. When we saw that bandaged right hand we knew that it was him that tried to steal Kylie's cross. We thought it highly likely before seeing his bandaged hand, but seeing it confirmed our suspicions. I think he got a 'hot hand' from the cross. They did actually come close to pulling it off ..... and we'll never know for sure what happened to stop them, but I think its somehow related to that old hymn, 'Mighty is the Power of the Cross'. We found their passports and plane tickets. They were all headed for the Bahamas .... had flights out of Knoxville."

"And speaking of the cross," Fred said, "I bet Kylie is missing it. You could just feel the closeness he had developed for it."

"Yeah," Bert answered. "But as young as he is, he seemed to well understand that he just couldn't keep it. And he seemed actually pleased that Randy was made its caretaker. Kylie told me he looked forward to going to Lexington to see the cross when its ready to go on display. Carolyn and I plan to take him on its opening day."

Fred said, "From what I understand the boy is certainly well taken care of, and will still even retain ownership of the cross."

Bert replied, "Yep. He's well set. I've never had a judge move so fast to approve anything. We got approval 2 hours after my request for dispensation of the unclaimed moneys in the bank vault. The system can move fast, but not often. Likely related to how good everyone felt about the way things happened with both the bank holdup and the golden anchor cross."

"The story on that beautiful cross was something for the ages .... literally!" said Fred. "How fortunate things worked out that Pastor Bell knew Randy Peters, and that they were able to get to the bottom of things. People around here are still scratching their heads trying to realize that such a thing was found right here in Harlan County! Have all the media and the tourists left Wallins?"

"Yeah," Bert replied, "we kept a patrol car there until

the middle of last week, but things remained pretty much under control. By this past weekend all seemed back to normal. I'm sure a few people will continue to wander in to look around in the woods thinking they might find gold, but I don't think it'll cause any problem."

Fred asked, "Speaking of Wallins, I understand Maggard's Grocery put up a CLOSED sign. That right?"

"Yep, ole Pretty Boy couldn't stand the heat from loosing that 3.5 million dollars. He and Trigger took off to parts unknown, but ole Fatso got a job working at McDonalds. I think he works the drive-through window. If you need to hear an elephant joke, just order a Big Mac at the drive through."

"So Kylie and Carolyn are doing fine?" asked Fred.

"They sure are," said Bert. "I think without Snake around they'll just continue to do better and better. They are both quite active in church at New Hope with Pastor Bell. The Lord does provide."

Fred stood, and said, "Boys, today the coffee's on me."

Bert and Ape stood. Bert said, "Thanks Fred, guess we'll get back over to the office to see what's up with Preacher Puss."